MANIC LOVE

MANIC LOVE

An Unwanted Inheritance
of Mental Illness

BRENDA WEBB JOHNSON PH.D.

Manic Love

Copyright © 2021 by Johnson, B.W.

Published by:
Webb Johnson LLC
www.maniclovebooks.com

Cover design by Glenn D. Johnson, Jr.
Proofreading by Ryan O'Neal, Jr.

Printed in USA

ISBN: 979-8-9880426-0-0 (Print)
ISBN: 979-8-9880426-1-7 (Digital)

Library of Congress Control Number: 2023907603

CONTENTS

PROLOGUE

"Daddy's Dead"

²¹ "You have heard that it was said to those of old,
'You shall not murder; and whoever murders will be liable to judgment.'

— MATTHEW 5:21 —

The phone rang in the middle of the night, it was Franklin's sister screaming in the phone.

"Daddy's dead! Daddy's dead!" Franklin was silent and just held the phone as he quietly sobs.

Franklin did not say anything sitting there as if in shock, so I took the phone but only heard the words "knife", "blood", "bathtub."

I knew my mother-in-law had finally snapped. My sister-in-law, Charlotte, is animated anyway but right now she is hysterical, scream-ing, and crying. Franklin is more reserved in general and he is clearly shaken but sitting quietly, fighting back his tears with a bewildered look on his face as he sat staring at the wall.

Franklin and I had been married 20 years by now. We married when we were just 19 years old. Although I knew of him, went to school with his sisters, and had classes taught by his mother, we didn't actually start dating until a year after high school. I was actually dating

vii

one of his best friends my senior year of high school whom I would actually marry against my will since I didn't know anything about birth control. Regardless, Franklin dropped out of high school before graduation anyway so he could sneak into the Air Force. We wouldn't see each other again until after my short-lived, failed marriage.

Twenty years and five children later, I sit here terrified and in disbelief about my life, worried about my husband, in fear for my children, my grandchildren, and sometimes, especially now, I even fear for myself.

My name is Virginia Hendricks, and I married a charismatic man who was diagnosed with bi-polar disorder almost 10 years earlier. My husband's mother who was diagnosed with schizophrenia, had likely just killed her preacher husband of 40 years.

My father-in-law was the Presiding Elder of the Indianapolis district for the AME Zion Church, so his wife was also an AME Zion district first lady. The Presiding Elder oversees all of the Pastors in the district and the First Lady is typically a leader when it comes to Women's Missionary Societies within the district and helps with special events and support a variety of ministries and ministry leaders.

At that moment, the reality that my father-in-law may have been murdered by his wife was settling in my mind. I was calm on the outside, trying to be strong for Franklin, but I too am in shock and I could feel my heart beating fast. The details were sketchy, and the family was in crisis, so I knew we had to pack up the kids and head to Indianapolis for more information and to prepare for a funeral.

My mind started racing, thinking about all I had to do to get the kids ready to go while remaining calm and being supportive of my husband. I grabbed a few suitcases and started throwing things in them for Franklin and I.

In the back of my mind all kinds of things started popping up. I knew or at least was told that Franklin had homicidal ideations before so I couldn't help but worry if this was in my future as well. Franklin wanted to kill a couple of his female coworkers who made him angry and I never did find out what they did to make him so mad. Why didn't I ask any questions back then? I don't know how he planned to kill them, but the fact that he would tell anyone that he wanted to kill another person was scary. Back then I brushed it off as just a non-serious statement made in the heat of the moment, but now, in light of this situation, that story just popped into my head and gave me pause. What about my kids? Is this their future? Will they or I be in any potential danger staying with Franklin? How did I end up in this mess?

Reverend Hendricks was the one person in the world who understood what I am going through with Franklin and now he is gone! In the midst of my panic, I fell to my knees and started to pray.

1

Virginia

I grew up in a small rural town off Highway 17 called Millry, Alabama. When I say rural, I mean red dirt roads rural where everyone knows everyone, and the old-timers prefer to keep things exactly as they are. Today, that same red dirt road remains in front of the home I grew up in and sits there as if in a time warp. The entire town has a population of less than 700 people, only 2% of the population is Black. The primary industry is farming and lumber production. I guess you can say progress continues to bypass that part of Southwest Alabama but perhaps that is by design. Millry is true small-town American living where everyone knows everyone, the air is clean, the stars are clear, and the pace is slow which means less stress.

My family, the Langstons, ran a farm, primarily growing sugar cane. Most of my relatives have never left Alabama and they may or may not have a high school diploma although it was not viewed as a requirement in those days. Three of my siblings left home for college but none of them finished. I would have loved to have had that option, but as the oldest it was not presented to me. I don't think anyone ahead of me knew how to open that door. My mother's youngest brother provided opportunities for my younger siblings when he started working at Tennessee State, while I was expected to help my mother in the house. As the oldest, and the only one with a different father, I not only felt like a mother to my siblings but also as if I didn't belong. I dreamed about getting as far away from there as I could possibly run.

As a teenager, I may have only been 5 ft 4" tall with beautiful smooth wavy hair down my back, but I had a feisty attitude. My father was White, and I was so fair skinned that if they didn't know my family you would have thought I was White. I think my feisty attitude came from always being on guard for the looks, the uncertainty on the faces of White people when they saw me, and comments like

"I wonder why that little White girl is always with those Black people".

Or the resistance on the faces of Black people who knew who my mother was but not my birth father and would sometimes say

"I bet she was raped by that White man".

I know my mother heard the gossip and I can only imagine how hard that had to be for her.

I was the starting point guard on my basketball team, loved to fish, and hated being forced into a traditional role of a woman in the 50's. My father did not think women should fish so I had to sneak off alone to enjoy that hobby. On the basketball court it was like I was getting all of my aggression out which actually benefited my team, and we were champions for my final two years of high school as no other Black team in the state could stop us.

My biological father was White and when news broke about my conception, there was fear for both of them because it was illegal to have interracial relationships. There was no way a White family in rural Alabama was going to allow their son to have a Black child by someone who used to clean their family home. During that time, if the authorities found out about the relationship, both parents could have been arrested.

My mother was a soft spoken, but very strong woman and we called her "Muh". She was just 18 years old and worked for the Roger's family in Bigbee, AL as a live-in housekeeper. Bigbee is about 10 miles away from Millry but in Washington County, however, the city was so small that it was not included in the census. My father, Gilbert, was 20 at the time of his relationship with my mother and although my mother never talked about him, I am told that he was a very kind and gentle man. He stood about 6'2" tall with a slim build and had sandy brown hair. Although racial segregation was the rule, Gilbert made friends easily and he was social with Black people in the city and had a few Black friends at the plant where he worked. Since my mother lived with the family and they were close in age, they became friends when she finished her work. His parents owned a local retail store in Bigbee, so they were not home a lot leaving plenty of time for "socializing" between the two young adults.

It was not easy for my mother as a young pregnant woman. When she started to show, she was forced to move out and was met with hardship and rejection from her family. Her mother, Vivian, had a husband at the time who was not Muh's father, and he refused to let her stay there because she was pregnant. She then went to her Aunt Martha's home, then Aunt Nannette, Aunt Asther, but all of them refused to let her stay with them. Muh was out on the street all alone and pregnant.

Understandably, most people were afraid of what the White people in town would do to her and her baby so they were afraid to let her stay for fear that they too could get hurt. She went to a friend, Mrs. Patricia Thomas, who would have let her stay but just did not have any room in her home. She was finally welcomed by Cousin Joan and her husband Lester "Brute" Sampson and she stayed with them until I was born.

Cousin Joan was the local midwife who lived down the road from where I grew up. I actually stayed with her a lot when I was young and maintained a strong relationship with her throughout my life. She would end up delivering 1,016 kids in three counties in rural Alabama over her career as a midwife including my firstborn, Charles.

Rumor had it the Rogers' wanted to raise me as long as I "looked White" so my Cousin Joan and a neighbor, Mrs. Sweet, made it a point to hide me when they came around to see me. I was indeed very fair skinned, with jet black hair below my shoulders that had a slight natural wave to it. Although modest, I know I was quite attractive and drew attention from many suiters. I could certainly pass for White and in fact did from time to time to get jobs.

The Rogers' brought money for food and diapers to Muh when I was an infant. Other members of their family tried to visit as I got older as well. I was told my father would send money to my mom to help care for me, at least when his dirty co-workers didn't pocket it for themselves. As time went on, his family eventually told my mother that my father died in the military. However, he is also believed to be one of the two White men that I remember seeing from time to time at my bus stop. They would watch me get on and off the bus and I could hear one of them say

"There's my girl"

The men never approached or tried to talk to me, but I knew he was talking about me. Although I never met my biological father, we would find out several years later, after his death, that he had raised a family in a nearby city. I am hurt that I never had the opportunity to know who my father was when he was living. I remember asking my mom who my father was as an adolescent, but my questions were never answered. In hindsight, I guess I understand why. It had to be just as hard if not harder for her, especially since we will never know the whole story.

I suppose the White side of my family could not have been all that bad as they were willing to raise me had my mother agreed to hand me over and allow me to grow up White. For fear of losing me however, she decided to hide me for several months to make sure they didn't try to force that issue as I certainly could then and still now can pass for White.

Looking back, I now know I did know my White grandparents because we continued to go to their store in Bigbee. I remember them always being friendly and giving me extra candy. I guess they continued to support me and my mom in the best way they could and in ways I will never know.

2

The Langston's

Honor your father and mother so that your life will be long on the fertile land that the lord your God is giving you

— EXODUS 20:12 —

My stepdad, Wallace Langston, was a rough around the edges, loud talking, boisterous laughing, heavy drinking man, with rough working man's hands. I called him "daddy". He stood 6 feet tall and weighed about 240 pounds. He was rarely clean shaven so anytime he hugged me his whiskers would scratch my cheeks. He was firm when it came to discipline, but we all knew he loved his family deeply and worked hard to provide for us and keep us safe.

Farming required hard long hours on the job and so he was up before daylight and worked until sunset day in and day out. Although we grew all of the food we needed, daddy farmed sugar cane and sold the stalks at market to make sure he could feed and clothe his very large family. He would keep some cane stalks for us and the best tasting cane syrup you could imagine would be made right at home.

Since farming was unpredictable at times, a steady income was challenging. Having a family of eleven to feed daily seemed to create a lot of stress for daddy. My mother, Voncile, was a homemaker that did not add additional income so if we were short, he would become angry and take it out on anyone in his path, usually my mother. Sadly, it happened often.

My mother had beautiful smooth coffee brown skin with long dark silky hair and stood 5'10" tall. I think she had native American traits. She delivered ten children although one died from pneumonia during his third year of life. Muh was an excellent cook, homemaker, and mother. She made her role seem easy and truly demonstrated the Proverbs 31 woman.

It always broke my heart to hear daddy coming in the house loud talking because that was a clue that he had been drinking. When he was loud, I knew drama was likely to follow. Muh did all she could to protect us from his wrath, especially me since I was his only stepdaughter and he reminded her of that often. However, when he was sober, he was a wise and loving man and the only man I will ever call "daddy".

As the eldest of my mother's nine children, I had extra responsibilities beginning at a young age. Besides helping in the fields, and with the chickens, pigs, and cows, I also had to help my mother with my younger siblings. To help with my school supplies and clothes, I had to go to a neighboring field and help pick cotton. I would have to go pick cotton before school and man was that hard labor. After school I was helping at home with my siblings, so I felt like I was constantly working. With very little options, you do what you have to do but oh how I longed to have different options.

There were six girls and two boys in our family. Three of the girls in the family were light-skinned and the other three were darker yet seemed to have a problem with the three of us. There always seemed to be something different in how they treated me but I guess it is because I did stand out in the group. I must say I was quite attractive in my day so maybe it was all just jealousy or maybe something deeper. It used to bother me, but I had to get to the point where it really didn't matter, and I was only responsible for how I treated others. One difference I am sure they all noticed as far as discipline, was that my stepfather did not spank or yell at me like he did with all of my other siblings, but I don't know if that was his decision or my mothers, or perhaps he knew who my biological father was. Who knows what they were really thinking but the bottom line was we were family.

Oddly, I was the only daughter who played sports. I was pretty athletic and the starting point guard on my high school basketball team. I also participated in track and field where I did broad jump, long jump, sprints, and relays. Not really sure why none of my sisters participated in any extracurricular activities since we all seemed to be pretty athletic and strong from all of that work in the fields. Both brothers were pretty amazing basketball players though.

My oldest brother, Claude, was a lean six foot five inches tall handsome young man. He was humble and definitely a hard worker. Daddy was so hard on him. We all had to work in the fields before school, but he seemed to have higher expectations of Claude who usually put in more hours than the rest of us until Cecil was old enough to help.

Cecil is my youngest brother. He was a good kind-hearted kid with a mean streak, so no one messed with him. He was a slender 6' 4" and I think he looked and behaved the most like daddy out of all of my siblings. Every time I came home, there was another story about Cecil, usually funny but sometimes scary.

My sister, Sherri, was three years younger than me, beautiful and so smart. She was about 5'6" tall with beautiful chocolate skin and silky black hair. She was a little on the shy side until you made her mad. I think I could say that about several of my siblings.

My sister Lini was a genuinely nice person who I got along with better than most of my other siblings growing up. We would talk often just about everything. She shared my desire to get out of Alabama and see other parts of the world. Lini was able to connect with people so easily and always made others feel special. Lini could talk to anyone with ease and so you would think she was older than she really was.

Joyce was one of my closest sisters in adulthood. She was strong-willed, free spirited, and didn't let anyone push her around. She was about Muh's height standing five foot nine inches tall with freckles. She and Cecil had a similar personality and would not allow other kids to mess with them or anyone else they cared about.

Lois was my next sister who was also strong-willed. She was another sibling that came to live with us when stationed in Wichita Falls, Texas.

Judith was almost twenty years younger than me, so I was already married before she was born. We never kept her like so many of my other siblings. I think not having her come to stay with us interfered with us getting to know each other on a deeper level until much later in life. She was five feet five inches tall with very long beautiful black hair. She was beautiful inside and out and probably the best cook in the family.

Janice was the youngest and she was born after all three of my sons were born. She was the surprise child as my mother was in her 40's when she gave birth to her last child. She and Lenore, Lini's daughter, were almost the same age and grew up very close, more like sisters than cousins. Janice was five foot seven and probably the pretties of all the girls. She loved to have fun and had a contagious laugh. She loved fashion and like so many of us she wanted more than what Millry, AL could offer.

There were a lot of us, and I loved them dearly. I tried to do all I could over the years for my family, even from a distance. In spite of my desire to leave Alabama, it was home.

3

Franklin

Train up a child in the way he should go;
even when he is old, he will not depart from it.

— PROVERBS 22:6 —

Franklin Hendrick's often said he was from Indianapolis, Indiana but was actually born in Beatrice, Alabama. He grew up in Alabama, Florida, Kentucky, and Indiana because his father was a Methodist minister who pastored churches in those states. Franklin and I grew up very differently. He was from a middle-class family full of professional teachers and preachers. Most of his relatives were college educated and several had advanced college degrees.

As the oldest in the family, Franklin had a lot of pressure from his parents to fit their definition of "successful". His self-confidence, maybe a little arrogant, made him all the more attractive to me. Standing about 6' tall, 170 pounds, with a short afro, Franklin's large smile that showed all of his gums warmed my heart because it was so genuine. He seemed to know a little something about everything, and his rebellious nature was actually also appealing to me because he was willing to take the risks that I dreamt about.

When I met Franklin, Jr., he was home visiting on leave from the Lackland Air Force Base where he was stationed just outside of Fort Worth, Texas. He had been in the Air Force for about three years after sneaking in twice. This in itself was controversial as his mother expected, basically demanded, that Franklin, Jr. go to medical school from a young age. Strong-willed Franklin, on the other hand, was determined to be his own man and decided the military was more appealing than college so he was persistent to get in at any cost. His first effort to sneak off and join the military without permission from his parents failed when he forged his mother's signature at the age of 17. He made it to Texas for boot camp but when his mother found out she had the commander of the base return Franklin immediately. Franklin was so mad! He told me stories about his older relatives who were in the military and how every time he saw them in uniform, he just knew that had to be for him. The uncompromising preacher's kid, would not give up on that dream and settle into the life his mother wanted for him and he kept at it until he figured out a plan that would work.

On his second attempt to join the Air Force Franklin was able trick his father into signing by presenting the enlistment papers as paperwork his wife needed him to sign.

"Daddy! Mom asked me to get you to sign these papers. She wants me to bring them to her when I go up to visit."

"She did? He asked.

"Yes sir, just sign right here" Franklin said with a straight face although nervous inside. He counted on his father being too busy with his own affairs to stop and read what his wife needed him to sign. She had done this in the past and daddy typically went along with what she wanted instead of questioning which would result in a fight. He signed without looking and handed the enlistment paperwork back to Franklin and walked away.

Franklin immediately went to the recruiter's office and once again he was off to serve his country. This time when his mother found out, she still tried to get him returned but since it was a valid signature, there was nothing she could do. Of course, she was angry, but Franklin was off to Texas for boot camp, again. By the time I met him, he had been in the military for more than a year and his family was with him at the revival, so I guess she had no choice but to accept his choice for his life, at least that choice, before me.

Franklin was Reverend Hendricks's oldest son and like his father he was so smart and articulate. He was able to talk to anyone about anything knowing just what to say to make you feel immediately comfortable and connected. He also had a compassion for people and would genuinely care about what was going on with everyone he connected with. As the eldest son of a preacher he had pressure on him to not only represent his father but also impress his family on his mother's side. Franklin's family had very different expectations for his life than he had for himself. They, primarily his mother, wanted him to become a doctor and she was angry over his choices that she viewed as rebellious whenever she was not able to control him. Not only had Franklin disappointed her by going into the Air Force instead of college, as they planned, but he also married a girl from a low income family, who looked White, and I am sure that me having a child before marriage and then four more children with her beloved son didn't make her any more pleased.

Franklin had a mission to help people for as long as I can remember. He started participating in missionary work around the time our daughter, Carole, was born and he continued to participate in efforts through our churches in the Philippines, Taiwan, and Guam helping people with spiritual, social, and physical needs as able. We would host bible study in our home on a weekly basis in most of our duty stations. He may have been a rebellious preacher's kid, but he certainly lived his life demonstrating the presence of the Lord in his heart.

4

The Hendrick's

*Father's do not provoke your children
to anger by the way you treat them.
Rather, bring them up with the discipline
and instruction that comes from the Lord.*

— EPHESIANS 6:4 —

Franklin's family was middle class, probably upper middle-class for an African American family. They were home and landowners, college educated, and had several preachers and teachers in the mix. Unlike my family, they didn't seem to feel the struggles of the great depression growing up and enjoyed indulging in all that life could offer, within reason of course for a preacher and a teacher.

Franklin's parents met while they were in college. His father, Reverend Hendricks, graduated with a bachelor's degree in Religion from Daniel Payne College and his mother received her teaching certificate from Tuskegee Institute. They met at a school dance while in college. In that day Black professionals had to go where they could find jobs. They often lived apart during the school year but spent the summers together as a family.

Franklin was also the oldest of five. He had three sisters and one brother. Franklin's brother Jerome was always hanging with the kids who like to have fun. Jerome was about the same height as Franklin, but he had a different swag about him. He had dark deep eyes and wavy hair that he usually wore in neat short afro with the sides trimmed just right and a part to the side. He was also very handsome and a sharp dresser. Jerome was a lot of fun and he had a free spirit. He loved people and enjoyed adventure like motorcycle riding, dancing, and just enjoying friends and family.

The girls of the family always gave the appearance of perfection and knew how to work a crowd even as teenagers. They were all active in the church, attending Sunday school, bible study and worship services every week.

The oldest sister, Charlotte, was a friend of mine in high school. She was a great student and played on my basketball team. She was five foot five, and slightly stocky. She looked a lot like her mother but thank goodness she was more friendly, at least towards me. She had a high spirit with a contagious laugh that you couldn't help but smile or laugh with her. She would marry a slightly older man from Alabama and have eight kids of her own.

Franklin's middle sister, Frances, was almost 6 feet tall, slim, confident, and the true athlete of the family, lettering in three sports in high school. She was a lot younger than me, but I enjoyed watching her take over the reins of our championship basketball team after I left high school. She was outgoing and high spirited as well.

The youngest sister, Marilyn, was pretty young when I married Franklin, so I didn't get to know her until many years later. She 5' 5" tall and also caramel. She was very smart and made sure they all knew it. She was also very close to her mother.

Mrs. Hendricks was one of my high school teachers at Chatom High School. Our high school was in a neighboring city called Chatom, Alabama. Although Chatom was still small it was twice the size of Millry with over a thousand residents. It is the county seat for Washington County, and it is where we had to go for shopping. Franklin's uncle was the principal of my high school and a beloved son of Chatom. He brought his sister in to teach English when I was in high school.

My mother-in-law made it clear from the way she talked to me that she never liked me. Sometimes others could see it in the way she gazed at me as if she was burning a hole right through me. I never did find out why she had such contempt. Maybe because my family was poor, maybe because I looked white, or maybe no one would ever be good enough for her son. Nevertheless, I was never comfortable around her, I was never made to feel welcome in their home, and I made sure to limit my time around her and I would never be alone with her.

Franklin describes his mother as controlling and powerful. That is an understatement and yet their family held her up on a pedestal in spite of how mean she appeared to the rest of us. She certainly had an interesting life as an African American educator in segregated America. She spent her career teaching in Alabama, Florida, Indiana, and spent some time teaching in South Dakota on an Indian reservation. She also authored a children's book and contributed to a high school math book.

I know both of Franklin's parents were intelligent and well educated but I never understood how she could be a first lady of a church and spit such venom at people like me. I guess the Bible is right in Matthew 23:28 when it describes the people who appear to be righteous on the outside but full of hypocrisy and wickedness within.

That's how I see those who are holier than thou. Little did I know her behavior was connected to her struggles with schizophrenia and her refusal to get treatment. I wasted a lot of years being angry and avoiding her because stigma prevented that disclosure.

Franklin's family always seemed to be totally devoted to their mother's side of the family, the Cunningham's. The Cunningham's were a strong and proud family and Franklin was close to several of his aunts and uncles on that side of the family. They were also upper middle class and well educated. They were united in extending the stigma of mental illness and hid the reality of the serious mental illness that presented its head from time to time within the gene pool. Franklin had a mother, an aunt, and a cousin with schizophrenia and a first cousin with bipolar disorder. At least that we know of. Stigma runs deep so we probably will never know the true presence or impact of mental illness within this family, but we certainly have to be ready for what may occur in the generations that follow.

5

Reverend Franklin Hendricks, Sr.

"Honor your father and your mother, that your days may
be long in the land that the LORD your God is giving you.

— EXODUS 20:12 —

I know very little about my fellow caregiver, The Reverend Franklin Hendricks, Sr.'s extended family. We visited his sisters in Montgomery on a few occasions but he nor they talked much about family history and they never had any family reunions. That side of the family was a bit of a mystery.

It turns out Reverend Hendricks was adopted by his aunt Edith on his mother's side. His Aunt Edith was a preacher's wife and they lived in Montgomery with their three children, Joanne, Judith, and Samuel. My father-in-law was raised as their own, and his biological parent's identity was never shared with him until he was an adult.

Reverend Hendricks was groomed to be a preacher from a very early age within the AME church. He was expected to follow his adopted father and their long line of Hendricks preachers into the ministry. His adoptive father was Reverend Wesley Hendricks and his adoptive grandfather was Reverend Vernon Hendricks. Vernon Hendricks was actually born a slave in 1818 but would become a minister later in life. My father-in-law was expected to follow in their footsteps, in spite of not being Wesley's biological son.

Some may say "generational curses" are inherited from our fore-fathers but actually poor Franklin, Jr. couldn't catch a break from his genetic inheritance from both of his parents. From sexual immorality on his father's side to mental illness on his mother's side, Franklin, Jr. would certainly follow in their footsteps.

Reverend Hendricks biological mother was a prostitute and living in the streets of Montgomery, Alabama when she left him to be raised by her sister right after he was born. He never had the opportunity to have a relationship with his mother and her story and location is still unknown. In spite of that, he was raised in a loving home and he loved his family dearly.

From the beginning, Reverend Franklin Hendricks, Sr. did every-thing right. He studied under his father to understand the ways of the AME church, read the AME doctrines, and attended all of the church conferences. He read and studied the Word, participated and served in a variety of youth ministries, and then started sup-porting his father by helping with administrative duties around the church.

He attended and graduated from Payne College with his degree in Theology and he married a woman from an educated family to be his First Lady which was important to him because a First Lady of a church also helps the pastor shepherd its members. He was confident that a wife like Frances would help his career. After graduation, Reverend

Hendricks was immediately ordained and given an opportunity to serve in the AME church.

Reverend Hendricks and Frances waited eight years to start a family. Frances wanted to establish her teaching career and Reverend Hendricks was striving to serve to the best of his ability. He remained faithful, and served well by connecting with each of his congregants, getting involved in district church activities, building relationships with locally elected officials, paying attention to the political and social trends of the community, and seeking to have influence that supported the well-being and improvement within the Black community.

Reverend Hendricks was about 5'8" tall, had a short afro that was already slightly balding around the temples. He wore wire-framed glasses and smoked a beautiful handmade wooden pipe. I have never smoked but always thought his pipes smelled so good. Although gentle and caring by nature, Reverend Hendricks was a strict disciplinarian and believed that children should be disciplined and represent their parents well in public.

He was the primary caregiver for Franklin, Jr. when he was young and often, they would live in Kentucky while the rest of his children were in school with their mother in Indiana or Alabama for nine months out of the year.

Twenty years into Reverend Hendricks ministry, sexual immorality was exposed. Already a father of five and married to an independent professional woman away for nine months a year, temptation got the best of him and the good Reverend started and continued an affair with a young beautiful woman for many years.

This affair would end his career with the AME church once revealed to the Presiding Elder and Bishop in that district in Greenville, Kentucky. Fortunately, for Reverend Hendricks, he would find favor in the AME Zion Church.

He joined the AME Zion church but continued the affair that resulted in his youngest son's birth a few years later. That time his Presiding Elder and Bishop decided that it would be best to transfer Reverend Hendricks to Indianapolis so he could be closer to his wife and children.

Reunited with his family, Reverend Hendricks became the non-traditional caregiver for his family by cooking for and helping clean after the kids. As my mother-in-law continued to decline, he became her caregiver and protector as well. Her bizarre behavior would cause difficulties for him in the church and the community and he would always "handle" it and cover up her mental illness in the process.

In spite of any poor choices my father-in-law made along the way he was one of the nicest people I have ever met. He fought a long hard battle against generational curses attacking him and those attacking his wife. Just as he was planning to escape, it cost him his life. I believe, he was killed because he was going to leave.

He had married a woman from a strong influential family who would later be diagnosed with schizophrenia. His life was in constant turmoil and no one had a clue. Franklin's mother refused proper treatment for her mental illness and the symptoms of schizophrenia would often result in bizarre behavior ranging from threatening words towards others to running down the street naked on more than one occasion. He could not possibly have imagined he would actually lose his life to his wife. Who would ever think that could happen at the hands of your spouse?

6

The Revival

Won't you revive us again, so your people can rejoice in you?

— Psalm 85:6 —

I met Franklin at a church revival where his father was preaching on temptation and perseverance. It would take years for me to connect Reverend Hendricks's sermons as a way of dealing with his own struggles, guilt, and regret over the years he spent unhappy and waiting for the next shoe to drop.

Choir Singing:

"Look back and see how far we have come.
Look back and see how far we have come.
Through the sunshine, through the rain, through the …
Oh look back and see how far we've come."

The first night of the True Light Church revival was underway. The pews were full, the musicians were in rare form and the best choir in the church was performing. The majority of the church was on their feet clapping and singing along to this classic song. The preacher of the hour, Franklin Hendricks Sr., was the guest speaker for the revival. His schoolteacher wife, Frances, was in the front row, dressed in her favorite purple hat with a beautiful dress to match. She was a large woman standing about 5'10" tall and weighed about 250 pounds. She was brown skinned, dressed conservatively showing very little skin. Her hair was always in place and her jewelry was typically pearls. She was an extrovert who Franklin always described as overbearing and powerful. She was an accomplished educator with a master's degree and authored a children's book. Later in her career she would have difficulty managing jobs without the help of her brother, the principal at my high school in Alabama.

The Hendricks's five children were sitting towards the back of the church with their friends but within eyeshot and she would give them a stare if they got too loud. Reverend Hendricks's children were all within seven years of each other and all of them, except for the youngest, had their own reputation as typical preacher's kids. They put up a good face in church for the most part but often have a reputation outside of church as worldly and sinful. Some can't wait to escape the scrutiny of good church folks so they can do their own thing. Others turn their backs on faith all together when they hit adulthood. It's funny how preacher's kids are often at the center of gossip within the church and that had to be difficult for a typical teenager. It seems a bit unfair to always place such unrealistic expectations on them just because their father was called to preach. But I guess Reverend Hendricks, and all overseers in the church are held accountable for their kid's behavior and even the bible supports that righteous judgment. 1 Timothy 3:1-6 reads:

"If anyone aspires to the office of overseer, he desires a noble task. [2] Therefore an overseer[a] must be above reproach, the husband of one wife,[b] sober-minded, self-controlled, respectable, hospitable, able to teach, [3] not a drunkard, not violent but gentle, not quarrelsome, not a lover of money. [4] He must manage his own household well, with all dignity keeping his children submissive, [5] for if someone does not know how to manage his own household, how will he care for God's church?"

The Presiding Elder's kids were no different. Nothing too serious just typical teenager stuff like dancing, drinking, and card playing but seemed to keep people talking, kept the first lady on the war path, and the Presiding Elder on his toes.

7
Temptation and Perseverance

In the presence of God and Christ Jesus,
who will judge the living and the dead,
and in view of his appearing and his kingdom,
I give you this charge

— 2 Timothy 4:1 —

After the music, announcements, and offering, Reverend Hendricks steps up to the pulpit. Following his prayer, he directs the congregants to turn to 2 Timothy 4:2-3,

"Preach the word; be instant in season, out of season; reprove, rebuke, exalt with all long suffering and doctrine. For the time will come when they will not endure sound doctrine; but after their own lust shall they heap to themselves teachers, having itching ears."

Reverend Hendricks seemed to preach often about temptation and perseverance. Perhaps this is his way of dealing with his own struggles, guilt, and regret over the years. He was hiding the truth about his affair, he had a secret child, and he had to be tired as a caregiver. I can only imagine how hard it was for him to be a caregiver for the wife he loved while feeling too helpless to do anything about her mental illness. They were struggling in silence as stigma kept that diagnosis a secret. Perseverance was definitely a necessity in his life. His life as a Presiding Elder was already complicated and challenging to Sheppard a flock for a district but then when you have secret sins, a secret homelife, and likely feeling some guilt and shame, it had to be hard for him to truly give all of himself to his work.

The sermon title for today was "Perseverance: Its Price and It's Profit." Everyone loved to hear Reverend Hendricks preach. He had such charisma and a style that would keep your attention. Perhaps it was because his messages always kept it real and related real life to scripture to make the message stick beyond Sunday morning or in this case our week-long revival of messages. This sermon was using examples from the recent football game at the high school where a controversial call caused a riot in the stands and arguments on the field. One player was so outraged by the call he actually walked off the field like a spoiled brat. Since most of the congregants were at the game they could easily understand the example. Reverend Hendricks went on to relate that example to how the congregation of adults often act that way as well, regardless of our job or status in the community, management, or our politics. Even adults seek to not follow the rules, play fair or decide to quit. He went on to say

"The worst form of child's play is seen in the lives of those people, young and old, who have quit on life — those who for all practical purposes have given up on life. We speak here not only of those who slouch along the streets of skid row in spiritual death, but also the spiritual death that occurs in so many before the physical death. It often goes unnoticed. It is difficult to know just what caused so many of our young men and women to walk

away from their jobs or what word or action from a thoughtless family caused that husband or wife to decide marriage wasn't worth the effort. Or that young first grader who starts out bright-eyed and eager but somehow gives up learning by middle school. Is it a poor home environment, uninspired teachers? My message today is directed at life's drop out."

"Jesus beamed his gospel to those apathetic to life's exuberant way of living. He talked to them about being born again, new birth in fullness of life, redemption and salvation from their spiritual death. Jesus promised no easy way, no easy medicine. He was honest and open; the way to fullness of life was narrow, hard way – the Via Dolo Marilyn cross that he himself trod. One of Aesop's fables illustrated the Christian way of perseverance. It is the one of the crow and pitcher, where a thirsty crow found a pitcher with so little water left in it that it could not reach it with its beak. By dropping one pebble after another in the pitcher, the crow was able at last to b ring the water up to a level where it could drink. The water of life is ours in the same way. There is a price to pay to realize anything of value, any profit. The pebbles are the price, the water is the profit. Both are part of perseverance or patience. Babe Ruth accumulated many baseball records; he was the home run leader with 714 until Hank Aaron took the record. However, for Babe Ruth the price for that profit was that he held another record for strikeouts. Babe Ruth struck out 1,330 times in his career, which was actually beat by Reggie Jackson who played longer and totaled over 2500 strikeouts. However, it was noted that this weakness tempted Babe Ruth to give up the game on many occasions. Perseverance always has its price and it always precedes the profit. Even Michael Jordan will tell you that he missed over 9000 shots in his career and lost almost 300 games. 26 times he was trusted to take the game winning shot and missed. He believes his failures are why he succeeds."

"Carl Sandburg said, 'Life is like an onion; you peel it off one layer at a time and sometimes you weep'. Sandburg may have come to the insight through study of the man whose life he researched and wrote about:

Abraham Lincoln. Lincoln, the failure at fifty, was defeated for public office 16 times before winning his first election. What if he had not continued to persevere? But he did and after he began harvesting the profits, he said on one occasion: 'A person's own resolution to persevere is more important than any other thing.'"

As I said earlier, the Christian Way, in reality is a way of perseverance. One of the earliest Christians to recognize this and lift its truth is Paul. He lived and preached perseverance, persevering successfully over physical, spiritual, legal, political, mental and economic obstacles. He had no soft words with those who couldn't take it. You can just about open the Bible to any passage in his apostle's and read a pep talk on perseverance. We have selected one from the 2nd letter to the young Timothy. Listen to these phrases of perseverance from chapter 2 Tim 4: "I charge you…proclaim the message, press it home on all occasions convenient or inconvenient, use argument, reproof and appeal, with all the perseverance that the work of teaching requires…always be steady, endure suffering, do the work, fulfill your ministry…" Then Paul offers testimony to his own perseverance. "I have run the great race, I have finished the course, I have kept the faith…" That was the price. Then Paul mentions the profit of his perseverance: "And now the prize awaits me, the garland of righteousness which God awards me…"

I always loved hearing Reverend Hendricks preach. I remember this sermon hit home for me as I desperately needed perseverance. Life at home was hard and I did not see a future there. I knew there was more for me than helping my Muh raise my siblings. I was ready to run away and not look back.

8

First Love

*"Remember not the former things, nor consider the things of old.
Behold, I am doing a new thing; now it springs forth,
do you not perceive it? I will make a way in
the wilderness and rivers in the desert.*

— ISAIAH 43:18 —

After revival, all who wanted to stay, gathered in fellowship hall for a good home cooked meal. Unfortunately, I did not get in line to greet Reverend Hendricks as his wife was standing with him. Mrs. Hendricks was one of my high school teachers. She taught math and English for my last three years at Chatom High School. She had to be my least favorite teacher of all time. Not because she wasn't capable, she was very intelligent and accomplished. She just had her favorites and didn't mind making it known. She would smile at some students and frown at others. She graded my papers more harshly without explanation but would coach other students. The way she spoke to me in class made me not want to be there, so I would skip class or find a way to get out of going. As we left the sanctuary, I decided to avoid the unpleasant and awkward experience of her fake smile and kept it moving to fellowship hall to see if I could help with anything.

As usual, everyone could smell the wonderful cooking of Sister Elaine down the foyer. You could smell the fried chicken, collard greens, macaroni and cheese, and cornbread and it was enough to make your mouth water. The tables were already filling up with eager diners when I walked in. My mom and her sisters were helping to prepare and serve as they always did by placing the plates, silverware, and napkins in front of the food and getting the serving trays ready. I was just looking for a place to sit and relax for a change. To my surprise a seat was open next to Franklin Hendricks Jr., the wayward preacher's kid home on military leave, and he was waiting for eye contact to invite me to join him. Against my better judgment because I knew he was a charmer and a good friend of my former husband, I decided to take a load off anyway.

"Please have a seat Virginia", Franklin said as I walked near the table and he greeted me enthusiastically with that big beautiful smile of his.

"Why thank you Franklin", I replied. I was surprised that he seemed so happy to see me but again, he was a charmer. Franklin was not a stranger but not exactly a friend either. His sister and I graduated from high school together, so I had seen him around from time to time and we went out as a group maybe once or twice. He greeted me with a big smile as if we had been best of friends and went on to tell me about his new journey in the Air Force. I was surprised how easy it was to sit there and talk with him for so long. I was not much of a talker, but he had a way of pulling people in.

"You look especially beautiful today", Franklin said in a flirting way.

"Thank you", I replied with a half-smile and probably blushing.

"Did you enjoy the service today?" He asked with sincere interest.

"Yes, I always enjoy hearing your father preach".

He had such a warm and inviting smile, the kind that shows your gums and people say those smiles come from warm genuine people. And he made direct eye contact that caused butterflies inside, so I had to quickly turn away. He had just completed basic training and he sure did look handsome in that uniform. It fit him perfectly and he just seemed so comfortable and confident and proud of himself for wearing the uniform in service to his country.

"I am a temporary duty assignment for a couple of weeks. I will be heading back to Texas next week. I am stationed there for now, but my new orders should be coming soon, and I hope they send me somewhere good".

"How do you like the military so far?".

"I am loving it so far. Freedom, opportunities to travel, learning new skills. My current job is an aircraft mechanic. Never thought I would be able to do that but it's great to use my hands to support our pilots as they prepare to go and fight. Plus, this type of job could be used anywhere in the world".

"Wow, that would be great. I could only dream about getting out of here and seeing the world. Maybe I should join the military", Virginia replied.

Franklin just laughed.

'What's so funny?" I asked, almost insulted. "Don't you think women can serve in the military?".

"I apologize if I offended you, you are just too pretty and there are not many women in the military you know".

"Well, maybe more of us should sign up and help make it better," we both laughed.

I couldn't help but daydream about my own possible adventures but joining the military was not a choice I would seriously consider.

It was still the 1950's and you really didn't hear much about women in the military.

"Well you could always be a military wife and enjoy the same benefits", He said looking directly in my eyes without the smile.

I have to admit his excitement and energy made him much more interesting than I had remembered, and I was truly happy for him, but that comment left me speechless. I didn't know if he was directing that to me as a serious consideration or just making a general statement.

What seemed like a quick meal had actually turned into two hours and the fellowship hall clean-up was beginning. We talked and laughed about pretty much everything and everyone until Franklin's mother, Frances, abruptly interrupted us.

"Hello Mrs. Hendricks, good to see you" I said with a smile on my face hoping it would disarm her normal bitter self and possibly, for once, be kind.

"Hello Virginia"

Of course, she was not coming over to speak to me, she was all too happy to try and get her beloved son away from her least favorite student.

"Franklin, come let me introduce you to Cheryl, one of my favorite students from high school", her emphasis was on f-a-v-o-r-i-t-e as she looked at me instead of Franklin.

"Cheryl is getting ready to go to college and I think you will be pleased to meet her".

It was obvious that his mother preferred Cheryl to someone like me whose family was not as affluent as hers. Franklin felt my uneasiness and respectfully advised his mother that he was in the middle of a conversation and he was certain there would be another time to meet Cheryl. Cheryl was a nice girl, very smart, a little cute but of course I think I am much more attractive. She was a little on the heavy side and was standing across the room looking a little awkward observing our interaction. I appreciated Franklin's efforts to be respectful of my feelings but also knew how demanding Mrs. Hendricks could be.

"Come on here Jr and meet Cheryl; it will only take a minute".

Franklin rolled his eyes and respectfully went to meet Cheryl, but quickly returned to continue our talk and then stayed to help us clean up fellowship hall and prepare for the next night of revival. He was growing on me instantly. At the end of the evening

Franklin said, "would it be ok if I come by your house to see you tomorrow?"

I was surprised but excited on the inside while staying calm on the outside. I did not want to get my hopes up too high, but I simply said, "Sure".

For the next week, I saw Franklin every day until he left for Texas. We would talk for hours on the porch about everything and even in silence it was just …. Comfortable.

I could talk to him freely about anything, my family liked him, and his stories outside of Alabama gave me hope. I didn't want him to leave but the Air Force owned him now and he had to either return to duty or go to jail. After that evening, to protect my heart, I didn't think much of it and figured I would never see him again.

To my surprise, he returned every weekend to visit me, as long as he could get a pass. We continued our courtship, mostly just sitting and talking or walking and visiting friends and family.

As a 19-year-old in search of a life, the attention he was bringing my way melted my heart. This was actually the first time I had every truly been pursued like this by any man and deep down I hoped it would be the last.

9

Our New Adventure

Then the Lord God said, "It is not good that the man should be alone; I will make him a helper fit for him"

— Genesis 2:18 —

It didn't take much for Franklin to convince me to leave Millry for a chance to possibly see the world as a military wife. I had lived here all of my life and knew there was so much more out there to see and do and there was nothing exciting waiting for me here. He was offering me an opportunity for real love, adventure, and not to mention relief from babysitting and cleaning up after a bunch of kids that weren't even mine.

Before I met Franklin, I was forced to marry Joshua, my high school sweetheart. He was my first love and in ignorance to the consequences we ended up conceiving a child. He and Franklin were actually pretty close friends in high school. Joshua as about 5'10" tall, stocky build, brown skinned with a short afro and a true country boy. He was a football player and we hit it off socially, but I don't think it was a true love connection. Joshua was happy in Alabama. He didn't have a lot of desire to get out of here and see the world, he was comfortable and that's ok. We had a true shotgun wedding with my dad holding the gun. That marriage lasted about a week before I ran back home pleading for them to let me leave that entanglement. After that I had no choice but to explore my options.

I couldn't afford college even though I dreamed about having my own career. Most women of my time were homemakers and I couldn't see that being enough for me. When I was in high school, I didn't have anyone to talk to me about options like college and I didn't know what I didn't know. Jobs were scarce in our small community and so a lot of us would have to leave our family to find jobs.

I did move to Birmingham briefly to stay with a cousin. I left my infant son Charles with my Cousin Joan. She agreed to watch him so I could get settled in up there. I was able to get a job at a local diner but only because they thought I was White. I worked there for about a month before quitting because I couldn't take watching Black patrons served from a window because they were not allowed to sit in the dining room with White folks. Here I was a Black woman taking orders and serving White patrons in a diner, but I couldn't serve other Black patrons because their skin was darker than mine? I may have looked White, but I was a Black woman just trying to make enough to support me and my infant son. I needed to explore something beyond the small two-bedroom home crowded with two adults and eight siblings. I loved the freedom of living with just one other person and working to have my own money but I could not continue working in these conditions and since I couldn't find another job quickly after quitting, I decided to go back home and not be a burden on my cousin. Besides I really missed Charles.

I had only been home for about a week before meeting Franklin. My son Charles was barely 6 months when we met, and Franklin immediately accepted him as his own. In fact, he would eventually adopt him into our family.

Our quick impulsive decision to get married meant we would go to the courthouse, no wedding, no dress, not even a ring. We took his younger brother, Jerome, and his wife, Tyana, across the Alabama border into the state of Mississippi to witness our marriage as we prepared to leave my lifelong home as man and wife. At the time, although still exciting, there was something about a traditional wedding that always stuck in the back of my mind. The image of a woman where all of her friends and family make her the center of attention if only for one day was a once in a lifetime fairytale that I now would not experience. Given my circumstances of already having a shotgun wedding and a young son, it really didn't bother me. I didn't get much attention growing up with such a large family so that one special day being walked down the aisle by your father is supposed to be one of the most special days of your life. For us, today, we went to a courthouse in an unfamiliar town with witnesses I barely knew, signed some papers and it was done. It was still a special day that I will never forget. I was now Mrs. Virginia Hendricks. We were married, packed, and heading off for Texas in less than two months after meeting at that church revival and I had no plans of looking back. I was finally off on a new adventure.

The military was different and not easy to get used to. We had to complete a ton of paperwork to get me added to his military record as his wife. We needed birth certificates and marriage certificates. This was all new for both of us, so we had quite a time navigating the paperwork. The military was resourceful and helpful with getting everything we needed.

As a military wife, you have free medical care and access to everything that the base has to offer. Tax-free shopping for food, clothing, and household needs was in the base exchange store and the commissary where we bought our groceries. Family housing was available on most of the bases we were stationed on and if not, a housing stipend was provided to live off the base. Cheap recreational activities like fishing lakes, bowling alleys, clubs, and sometimes golf was available on most bases. Medical and dental services were also right on post. There was very little need to leave the base. I was really excited about the opportunities to travel around the world when our family was allowed to join Franklin. When we couldn't move, I would just go home for a while.

The military family becomes your family and we spent a lot of fun nights and weekends with other young couples in search of adventures. The first friend I met when arriving in Texas was Mary Patterson. She was also a newlywed and she and her husband Gene were starting their military marriage adventure as well. Mary and I hit it off instantly. She was from North Carolina and one of the nicest people I had ever met. She was about 5'6" tall with medium length hair that she kept pulled up most of the time. She was a great listener, loved to laugh, and just made you feel so welcomed every time she saw you. Most of my friends before now were typically family members since our small town, school, and church were filled with a lot of distant relatives.

Since Mary and Gene had been on post longer, she showed me around and helped me understand military life. During the week we spent a lot of time together and on the weekends the four of us would get together for a movie, dinner or an evening at the enlisted club.

Our first apartment in Texas was off post. It was a small two-bedroom apartment. Franklin was living in the barracks before we got married and there was no married housing available at the time of my arrival. We were only a few miles away from the Base and it was small but perfect for our new yet small family.

Since Franklin worked so much, he had no choice but to teach me how to drive. I never had the opportunity to get a license when I was in Alabama, so I had to learn in Texas. Franklin and I would have our first fight during this lesson, and he made me so mad one day I almost walked home.

"Virginia!", Franklin yelled causing me to slam on the brakes of the car.

"Why are you yelling at me!", I asked with a trembling voice.

"I thought you were about to run off the road!", he said looking at me as if I was one of his soldiers.

"I was not that close to the edge Franklin! You scared me to death", I cried.

"How could you have gone all of these years without learning how to drive? Hell, most kids in the country learn how to drive way before they are 16", he chuckled.

"Well, Franklin, you know daddy was not going to let me drive his truck or his tractor. He did not let women do those things!",

"I wish he had because you are about to give me a heart attack".

"Just forget trying to teach me then Franklin", I said as I pulled the car over and got out.

"Come on now Virginia, you don't have to be like that".

"Just take me home Franklin!", I said as I got in the passenger side.

We drove home without talking anymore and I was so mad at him for thinking this was funny. Nevertheless, I passed the driving test on my first try and now I was able to go to different places during the day while Franklin drove a bicycle to his office on the base.

Franklin's family liked nice things and didn't worry about money. My family pinched every penny to make it last and did not spend foolishly. This would become a challenge for our marriage. He furnished our small apartment with very nice furniture and I felt it was too much because I was not used to nice things. I was a stay-at-home mom, so he did not involve me in financial decisions early in our marriage. I just couldn't imagine that a new service member could afford some of what he bought but I was not sure. I was such a young and naïve new wife.

I had ambitions but my plans were altered early in life with limited opportunities in my small rural town and now as a wife of a military service member with an infant, I was not in a position to make any personal plans. Our life was dependent on the decisions of the Air Force. Most families expect to move every 2-3 years. I had dreams of going to college and leaving Alabama but never saw it as an option. At least my desire to leave Alabama was accomplished thanks to the military.

This was my opportunity to see the world. I heard stories from other military wives about all of the places they had lived in and I would often daydream about the new adventure we were starting. I would think about countries that I hoped he would get assigned but that decision was not ours. I not only wanted to leave Alabama, but I looked forward to leaving the United States and soon that too would become a reality.

We were only 19 and looking back we probably were not ready for marriage. I came into the marriage with an infant son and Franklin was not ready for that level of commitment. For the first six years of our marriage, I was home with three young sons taking care of their needs and trying to be a good wife while he spent most nights at the non-commissioned officers club drinking and not coming home until just before dawn. We would go out together occasionally, but having young children made that difficult at times. He, on the other hand, often went out with the boys. I was home trying to be the good wife, cooking, cleaning, and waiting for him until I couldn't wait anymore and would drift off to sleep angry and in tears. He would creep in at some point smelling like whiskey and smoke and would be fast asleep when I woke up. We fought so much during those early years it is a wonder how we lasted for thirty-six years of marriage.

One evening, Franklin was in the bedroom getting dressed and smelling good, so I asked him,

"Where are you going now?"

"You know I always go to the enlisted club on Friday night with the boys."

"You mean Monday-Sunday", I said sarcastically.

"They are closed on Sunday", he smirked.

"Franklin, I really wish you would spend some time at home with me and the boys. You work all week and then you are off again with the boys most nights. When are we going to get some of your time?"

"Virginia", he said sincerely, "Who will keep the boys if we go out together? You need to take care of them", he said as if he had no responsibility for caring for them and then he just walked out the door.

I was basically a single parent for the first six years of our marriage because when he was home he was sleep or hung over and then would pull himself together to get up and go to work. What have I gotten into? This is not what I was hoping for but what can I do at this point? The alternative was Alabama and that was not going to happen, so I had to figure this out. I got on my knees, turned to God, and began to pray daily for my husband.

Little did I know, Franklin, had also fallen into sexual immorality just like his father. I would later learn that he believed his drinking was born in guilt from hiding the fact that he had multiple affairs during the early part of our marriage. He was not just out with the boys. He had found several women while he was roaming the streets and had multiple sexual relationships. With each affair he would go deeper into his guilt and tried to avoid coming home because he didn't want me to know. I don't know why he felt he had to cheat on me, although we talked a lot, we were not the best at communicating our feelings. I don't know if it was influence from his friends or just him putting himself in a position to fall to temptation with the clubs and alcohol, but something had to change.

When we were about 25, Franklin changed. Although his father was a minister and he had an understanding of God, he says he was not truly a Christian because he didn't accept Jesus as his Savior, Master, and Lord. He did not repent from how he was living or treating his family until he confessed with his lips and believed in his heart that God raised Him from the dead and once he became saved, his life, our life changed. Our family life changed, and we were finally happily married. I believe in the power of prayer and have faith that my daily prayers for my husband helped to change his heart towards me and the boys. I also believe he was raised by his parents in the ways of the Lord and as Proverbs 22:6 says *"train up a child in the way he should go and when he is old, he will not depart from it."*

10

Raising Kids

*"Behold, children are a heritage from the Lord,
the fruit of the womb a reward"*

— Psalms 127:3 —

Franklin and I raised five beautiful children together. Our first three children were quick and back-to-back, barely more than a year between the three boys. I wanted a girl so badly but not enough to try quickly again because all three of my deliveries were hard on me. Never-the-less, we had two sons together in our first three years of marriage followed by our girls, four and seven years later. Franklin loved my oldest like his own and would eventually adopt him before our last child was born.

Franklin decided I would be a stay at home mom, at least until our youngest started elementary school. In reality, that was probably best as a military spouse. There were times when I would be left at home alone with the kids during his deployments so working would have been difficult. There were other times when I would choose to go home to Alabama for months at a time, especially towards the end of two of my pregnancies. Back then, husbands were not in the delivery room with their wives. Childbirth was always hard for me, so I found comfort in being home with my mom and Cousin Joan. Our third and fourth children were actually born in Millry alongside my mother. Our youngest daughter was the only childbirth Franklin was present to see. She was born in a military hospital in Albuquerque, New Mexico.

I was a traditional caregiver and put my heart and soul into caring for my family. I didn't particularly enjoy being a caregiver, but I was good at it. I cooked, cleaned, and sewed for my family which was a full-time job. There were eleven years between my oldest and my youngest, so I was a full-time homemaker for 16 years. I was devoted to my family but didn't always feel appreciated or fulfilled. I got very little help from Franklin when it came to taking care of our children, but he was the firm disciplinarian, sometimes too strict. The military held the service member accountable for their children so Franklin made sure his kids stayed in line so they would not make him look bad or interfere with his career in the Air Force. He was a strict disciplinarian and taught responsibility from a very young age. Each child had a space on the duty roster in the home and if they failed to do their chores there would be punishment. Franklin expected our children to carry out his commands immediately and showed very little patience towards them in the early years.

"Franklin, why do you have to be so hard on the kids?" I asked.

"If I give my boy a command, I expect him to spring up, like a jack comes out of a box, and start doing it at that moment."

"But Franklin", I pushed hoping to help him not be so hard on them, "sometimes, they are in the middle of something like homework, other chores, or watching TV".

"What they are participating in at the time of my command usually doesn't make any difference," he would say, sounding more like a drill sergeant than a father, "the order must be carried out promptly" he would insist.

"Don't you think that is a bit harsh?"

"This may seem harsh", he demanded as if he knew this was for the best, "but it was the way in which I was brought up. My father was very strict, and when he gave a command to me, it had to be carried out immediately or else I suffered the consequences which, in most cases, was a good whipping with switches"

"But Franklin", I insisted, desperately trying to change his mind, "you always said you didn't like the way your parents punished you and we talked about not repeating those things with our kids", I reminded him.

"I know, but If my kids linger when I give him a command, it will irritate me, and I will scold or punish him", he continued as though he heard nothing that I said. "I am so rooted in my parent's teachings that I find myself saying the same words, which my parents used, to my children when scolding them," he said, and I realized only God who could change him. "I responded to my parent's commands without hesitation and I expect my children to do the same", he insisted.

"Well, I don't agree. That is not what we agreed to for raising our kids," I would say over and over again, praying that one day he would understand.

We would have this conversation often over the years but always in private so not to show a hint of dissent to the kids. I think that is why they were so surprised when our marriage ended. They never saw us fight so they had a fairy tale image of what marriage was.

Eventually, after years of praying and probably his classes in Social Work, he was able to see the damage he was doing. Sadly, by then the boys were grown. At least the girls would benefit from the new relaxed approach and maturity from their father.

11

Our Children

"Children are a heritage from the Lord,
offspring a reward from him."

— Psalm 127:3 —

Our five kids were all so different. My oldest son, Charles, grew to be just under 6' tall with a medium length afro that would later recede. He had a large yet warm smile with a slight gap in his front teeth. He was a kind, loving, God-fearing man, with a big heart. He always followed the rules and got along with everyone. As the oldest he would try to hold the others in line but eventually found that task to be way too difficult. He was the one child we never had problems with at home or in school. He did his chores as soon as he got home, check it off on the duty roster, did his homework, and went out to play with friends consistently. Sadly, when he found out from his brother Lyle who his father was, he decided to finish high school in Alabama so he could get to know his biological father better. Although, this was heart breaking for me, I understood. Like his father, Charles loved Alabama and would remain there throughout his life.

Lyle, Franklin's first biological son, was light skinned and also just shy of 6' tall and skinny for a male. He would try everything he could find to gain weight, but it never seemed to work. He had an extra-large afro as teenager but started losing his hair at an early age which he was not happy about at all. He even went so far as to try hair plugs but that didn't work for long either. He was rebellious like his father and insisted on having his way and the last word. He wanted everyone to know he knew more than them, even his teachers, which did not often go over well. Unfortunately, that would result in expulsion a couple of times in elementary school after he insulted his teachers. He was fairly independent, factual, and critical of things he believed to be unjust. However, he was also driven and excelled in his school assignments. He often created animosity among his siblings and seemed to enjoy starting fights for no reason. Sometimes his behavior would be so ugly towards his siblings that Franklin wondered if he had a demon living within.

Lester was the social one, a talker, and the leader of the pact when his friends were getting into stuff, they had no business doing. Of course, it was never his fault. He also stood about 6' tall, athletic, with beautiful hazel eyes, and a stocky build. He was a little slower to mature and more focused on the here and now then seeing the big picture but it served him well socially. He struggled in school and often argued to prove he was right about everything even when he wasn't.

Carole was quiet but strong-willed. She would withdraw at times but then still try and figure out how to do what she wanted to do regardless of what we thought or what she thought we thought. She was only 5'4" tall and stocky. She struggled with her weight ever since childhood. She too, was very kind-hearted and loving and was probably more like me than anyone else. She also enjoyed cooking and sewing and knew how to show unconditional love to others.

Belinda was our tom boy, talked a lot as a small child and didn't let her siblings push her around. She is 5'9" tall, light skinned, and so skinny that I had to sew all of her clothes because the stores were not selling size zero back then. She didn't always listen well, but she was honest, trustworthy, and friendly. She too is strong-willed and independent but didn't pick up any of the domestic activities I tried to teach my girls. She always said she was never getting married or having kids anyway.

I learned that parenting these five unique children would require individual attention and all the unconditional love I could muster. Raising kids as a military wife had both benefits and challenges. Most military bases have secure recreation activities to enjoy with the kids so that helped me keep all five of them occupied. In spite of Franklin's deployments leaving me home alone, the military was like family and so other wives embraced and supported me by coming to the rescue as needed.

We moved as a family 10 times in 22 years both domestic and abroad. I remember vividly, that 36-hour flight to the Philippines alone with three boys between 2 months and 4 years of age. Not only was it hard to juggle the kids but the turbulence on that flight was so bad that ice cubes were floating in the air.

We were out of the country during the height of the civil rights movement and in the Philippines when Kennedy was assassinated in 1963. When we returned at the end of 1965 we had missed so much. That was quite a year with Malcolm X being assassinated, Bloody Sunday in Selma, Alabama followed by Dr. King's march to Montgomery that led to the Voting Rights Act of 1965. We left again in 1968 for Taiwan before Dr. King was assassinated. Not sure how I feel about missing such monumental events up close, but the news certainly traveled around the world for all of these events.

Franklin did well as a soldier, eventually becoming a non-commissioned officer retiring as a Master Sergeant. I am sure he would have gone further and stayed in longer had it not been for his genetic factors leading to his medical discharge. The first admission for treatment of mental illness would occur at the age of 30, shortly after the birth of our fifth child, Belinda. Overall, we had a blessed life together, and I firmly believe that his faith and walk with Christ has allowed him to sustain in spite of it all.

12

Spiritual Awakening

*"Because, if you confess with your mouth that Jesus is Lord
and believe in your heart that God raised him
from the dead, you will be saved."*

— Romans 10:9 —

You would have never guessed early in our marriage that Franklin was a preacher's kid. Don't get me wrong, he has always been a charming and loving man, but he also had a rebellious side and a desire to have a good time. He had a contagious laugh, huge smile, and knew how to make everyone he met feel special and enjoy themselves.

There were so many rules growing up with his parents that I think Franklin just became fed up with all of the prohibitions on playing cards, drinking, smoking, dancing, or listening to secular music that it was certainly no surprise that he made up for "lost time" in his young adult life. He went out to the club with his fellow service members as often as he could, even after we were married, until he finally became a born-again Christian.

The moment Franklin repented and accepted Christ as his Lord and Savior he became the husband and father I had been praying for. He described being in the middle of a field one night and says a bright light appeared and the ground began to shake. He stated that in the midst of what would normally be frightening, he felt an indescribable calm and he is convinced it was the presence of the Lord calling him to walk with Him. Of course, I was skeptical, thinking "yeah right" but there were no reported earthquakes on the news, no lightening reported, and no other strange sightings reported. I certainly saw a difference in him, and I was thankful. Talk about an instant change! At 25, he stopped smoking, drinking, clubbing, cursing, and the family started attending church faithfully every Sunday.

After the mysterious field experience, Franklin took his walk with Christ even higher through missionary work. While in the Philippines, he started missionary work at a Southern Baptist Church in Balibago. The church had mission chapels in many barrios, the name they use for small cities or towns. Franklin was responsible for the San Jose Mission Chapel. He taught Bible lessons there on Tuesday and Sunday. After teaching for approximately eight months, he was asked to teach an additional Bible class in the home of Mr. Gomez in Antipolo. Antipolo was located three miles from San Jose. He accepted Mr. Gomez's invitation and continued to teach in both locations until we departed the base in 1964. Franklin really enjoyed his tour of duty in the Philippines. He loved the fellowship, the food, appreciated the customs, and even learned some of the language while serving there.

In the community, there were special bible classes for children and adults at least once a month at the village in Antipolo, and another special bible study session that had the goal of teaching English to Chinese elders and students. I remember one night he and another service member did a sermon in a cane field near Ariella and there had to be almost 40 people who gave their lives to Jesus Christ.

On the base, he organized his Air Force team to donate to local families in need. One special family of a Taiwanese girl, Jao, left an impression on Franklin. Jao and her mother lived in severe poverty. Jao's mother was unemployed and struggled to care for her. Jao's father died and the family sought help through a local Christian organization where Franklin met her. He was the chief of the Taipei Aerial Mail terminal at the time while stationed on Shung Shan Air Force Base. When he told his unit about Jao and her mother, they all decided to visit the family in their one room shack that had a dirt floor. It was winter when they visited so the floor was very cold. The entire team was moved with compassion and decided to help the family. They sent two people to put a wood floor in her house and donated clothes, food, toys and money. After they delivered the donations, the team made a unanimous decision to continue to provide for Jao in hopes of contributing towards improved quality of life. They coordinated the effort through that Christian organization and every month the team contributed toward the support of Jao's family. That was just one family who benefited from Franklin's missionary work. Helping others was so natural for him that he was basically a preacher without the title.

After we left the Philippines, Franklin continued hosting bible study classes in our home every week for the next several years while stationed in the New Mexico, Taiwan, and Washington, D.C. He began forming his own outreach ministry by taking opportunities to reach out to military personnel. He would ask if they were interested in attending bible study at our house on Friday nights after work to learn more about the Word. He included military, non-Americans, and college students. There were many occasions where people would accept the invitation and then bring someone else along as well. My job was to prepare snacks and assist the women and children who attended.

Although Franklin never became a minister inside of a church, he certainly fulfilled his call to bring others to Christ. His missionary work would continue for several years and if he was walking with Christ his walk with the Lord made life at home loving and stable. Unfortunately, the unwanted inheritance of a serious mental illness began to surface.

13

First Hint of a Problem

"My peace I leave with you; my peace I give you.
I do not give to you as the world gives.
Do not let your hearts be troubled and do not be afraid"

— JOHN 14:27 —

Coming from a small farming town in Alabama and growing up in the 40's and 50's, I was so naïve when it came to mental health concerns. Black families certainly didn't talk about it but looking back I know there were issues that that were explained away as something else. Often, family would just dismiss the persons behavior as mean, weird, or a drunk.

"There's nothing wrong with Franklin", I remember his sister, Charlotte, saying often. "He's always been like that."

Even the bible minimizes the mention of mental health, but you do see it in stories throughout the bible with some references to "madness".

Regardless, stigma is real, and denial is in full effect in many families. The Hendricks family had a reputation to uphold, and mental health acknowledgement did not fit in with their image. The church was no better when it came to discussing or preaching about mental health. It just did not happen from what I could see.

I should have known Franklin's mother was not just mean. Her behavior was bizarre and downright weird at times. She would give us a look and we were not sure if she was mad at us or just trying to intimidate us, but it was so creepy that you would think she was burning a hole in our flesh. Sometimes you could not even understand what she was talking about in class and at times it sounded like she was mumbling in class. My solution was to just get a hall pass and find an excuse not to go to her class.

When Franklin started acting bizarre, I didn't know what to think and certainly didn't know what to do. A co-worker of his tried to warn me about Franklin's paranoid behavior in Albuquerque. I think he was careful on the words he chose to use, and I wonder if he was not allowed to share everything he knew. He mentioned how Franklin had become paranoid on the job and he was a little concerned. It would be years later before I would learn that he had actually threatened to kill a couple of his female co-workers during that time. To this day, I do not know why or what happened to spark such rage and I guess I am glad I didn't know then what I know now.

The first time I personally recognized behavior that caused great concern was after the death of his favorite Uncle Josiah. He was good to Franklin when he was a small boy living in Beatrice, Alabama with his Aunt Lucy. Uncle Joe died when we were still living in Taiwan so we could not attend the funeral. Franklin often became very angry when he thought about the way his relatives treated his Uncle Josiah before he died. He never confronted his mother or his uncle that was living in the home with Uncle Joe. So, he questioned the heart of many family members regarding how they failed to properly care for him when he needed their help. I think it hardened him regarding his family actually. In a strange way I think it also created some fear and anxiety about his own future.

"Franklin, I am so sorry to hear about the death of your uncle and I know it is hard to be across the ocean and not able to attend the funeral," I said as I could see the pain in his heart.

"Uncle Joe was very dear to me," he said. "When I was a child, he always had time to talk and sing to me. He played several musical instruments, and he would tell me various stories", he added. When I think of my childhood days, Uncle Joe is almost always included. He was crippled in those days and had to walk using a cane because of severe pains in his legs that they called rheumatism. Franklin reflected with empathy only felt by someone who saw his pain.

"He sounds like a very special man," I said trying to console him.

"Uncle Joe was confined to a bed, and he could not walk well at all by himself."

"Oh, that is so sad to hear," I said softly.

"My grandfather did a great job in taking care of him until he got sick and Uncle Joe's oldest son took him to his home to care for him. Those were happy days for Uncle Joe until his son decided to move to Ohio. He just didn't want to go so he moved in with his youngest son who built a one-room shack in back of his home and put his father in it. It was a dark place with a bed, and an iron stove that burned wood. That stove was used for heating and cooking his meals. He would tell me that often times, his grandson cooked his meals, washed his clothes, and changed his bed linens for him," Franklin shared.

"Do you think they did the best they could?" I asked not knowing much about that part of the family.

"No, I don't think any of them did right by him!" Frank sobbed. "He was my mother's brother. She went to see him on numerous occasions but did nothing to better his living condition. Uncle Joe's brother saw him frequently too but offered no help. My mother and her brother are school professors and one would think that they would offer financial assistance or any assistance because he was their brother."

"Oh, I see," I said as I continued to let Franklin vent.

"When I took leave from the Air Force, I would try to go to see him. He would tell me how his family mistreated him. Perhaps I have some guilt for not doing anything either. I was only on and they were there all of the time!", he began to cry as the pain of guilt and neglect flooded his mind.

"Franklin, you can't take that burden on yourself, and that anger will eat away at you. What else could you have done?", I asked as I tried to comfort him.

"I don't know", he whispered through the tears.

I had never seen Franklin grieve but this seemed a little extreme. His psychiatrist thinks this loss triggered his bi-polar symptoms. Like mental illness, the family seemed to want to hide Uncle Ike and they placed him in a small shack on the family property where he spent the majority of his days in isolation and alone. When Franklin learned about how he spent his final years on earth it seemed to have a depressing effect on him.

After his funeral, Franklin continued to seem down for quite some time. I thought it was just normal grieving, but it became much deeper. One day I walked into our bedroom and found Franklin laying out his best suit, suit, tie, socks, and shoes.

"Franklin, what are you doing?"

Franklin jumped and refused to talk to me. It was like he was in a daze and had the strangest look on his face. It frightened me but I did not know what to do.

His co-workers must have seen the same odd behavior, or he must have been exhibiting the same odd behavior at work, because shortly after, Franklin would be admitted into a psychiatric unit on suicide watch the following week.

I would later learn that the suit he pulled out was actually Franklin preparing for his own funeral and he planned on ending his own life that day. I did not know what to think or what to do other than pray.

14

The First Admission

"But when Jesus heard this, He said, It is not those who are healthy who need a physician but those who are sick."

— MATTHEW 9:12 —

Back then mental health doctors did not make it a practice to talk to family members. I was left in the dark, did not know what was going on with my husband, and did not know what to do to help. I had never known anyone who committed suicide. I can't even imagine what would drive someone to that level of hopelessness. All I knew to do was to pray and try to stay positive and encourage him. I continued to have faith.

Although I never thought about it before, I realized there is a hint of mental illness referenced in the bible. I also know how good intentioned church folk have a myth that suicide is unforgivable by God even though that is not clear in the bible. What is in there is how

King David wrestled daily at times with depression and he pleaded with God for healing and at least in Psalms 38:4 he sounds suicidal when he says: *"Jeremiah cursed his birth and questioned his existence"* in Jeremiah 20:14 and 18. Job grieved so deeply that he preferred death in Job 3:16. God answered their cries, and they became overcomers.

I believe God can turn anything around and I know Franklin has a heart for God. He knows the Word, and I am keeping my faith firm that God will turn this around for Franklin and use him for His glory. I want that for Franklin, and I prayed for that daily, I pleaded to God for that.

How was I supposed to talk to Franklin about this? What do I say when he comes home? What was I supposed to say to my children? What if he did it again? What if I had to be the one to witness it or find him? Is this what my future holds?

Franklin was the spiritual head of this home. He was a preacher's kid and taught the word to his family and anyone else. How could he lose his faith so much that he would want to just end his life? What is going on in his head? What have I gotten myself into? I love this man! I pray I have enough faith to help him through this.

Franklin received a new duty assignment and we had just moved into a new home In Washington DC on Andrews AFB when he was admitted due to suicidal ideations. Our youngest child was going to start school this year and I was looking forward to finding a job outside of the home. Just as we are getting settled in after that first admission, Franklin was hospitalized again to treat numbness in his left leg.

During this admission, Franklin was found sitting on a window ledge in a Neurology office where he was tackled by aides before he could jump. He was still struggling with the death of his Uncle Ike and little did I know that had left him spiraling into a deeper depression and anxiety. This bout with depression was rooted in fear of dying like his Uncle Joe alone and helpless.

This would be his second of three attempts or desires to commit suicide. He continued treatment for depression after this admission and tried a variety of medications including Elavil, Mellaril, and a series of electrocardiogram (ECT) treatments. The reality of his psychiatric treatment came along with a new set of fears that he would be forced out of the Air Force on disability.

I didn't know then that Franklin's physical symptoms were connected to his mental health. He started having chronic pain in his legs, his back, severe headaches, and he started having digestive problems. All these symptoms kept him attending multiple doctor's appointments with specialist who couldn't find any real problem other than irritable bowel syndrome. Some of his admissions were for physical complaints but he would also end up seeing psychiatrists as well. During Franklin's admission for back problems, he was given ten "shock treatments" over a period of four weeks for depression. After he came home, he told me about those treatments that sounded so horrible.

"Virginia, they convinced me to get ECT treatments while I was in there and the doctor had to put me to sleep during each treatment," he said. "Each time, I would have problems coming out of the treatments. I would wake up very quickly, could hear and see people talking, but I literally could not breathe. I thought I was going to die", he said.

"That sounds horrible Franklin!",

"I was so scarred I asked God to let me live and I would serve Him more faithfully, and that I would go on the spiritual conference that was coming up. I want you to come with me," he pleaded.

"Of course!" I said, happy he wanted me to be with him but still terrified he'd try it again.

He remained stable for a while but as time went by, Franklin continued to have anxiety stemming from guilt of not being a good father and unconfessed infidelity. Turns out he had never confessed to multiple affairs he had for nearly 15 years of our marriage, and the guilt was causing him increased distress. Although he claimed to be saved six years into our marriage, sexual immorality continued. We would later find out that my father-in-law, Reverend Hendricks, also had infidelities in his marriage, one resulting in a son about 13 years younger than Franklin.

After multiple doctors and admissions, Franklin would finally be diagnosed with manic depression before discharge. Manic depression was renamed in the DSM as bipolar disorder years later. Bipolar disorder is considered a serious mental illness (SMI) and is described as bewildering and sometimes hard to believe, at least for me. It is a biologically based brain disorder that causes fluctuations in mood from severely depressed to extremely excited. The swings are unpredictable, inconsistent, and episodic, not persistent. Being episodic means there are times of normalcy which makes it difficult for me to understand. I often wondered if he can truly control it or if he is playing victim and blaming bipolar for some of his bad choices and behavior. Since it is unpredictable, I feel like I am constantly walking on eggshells and never know when the next episode will occur.

Symptoms of bipolar include hyperactivity, irritability, excessive involvement in an activity, poor judgement, jumping around on topics while talking, inflated self-esteem, lack of sleep, becoming easily distracted, hyper-sexuality, illogical responses to questions, among other things. There may also be hallucinations, and delusions, including persecutory delusion which are similar to paranoia but targets people, usually me when it comes for Franklin. What is scary for me is that he doesn't even realize when an episode is occurring, and he will do things that he won't even remember later. Often, I tend to be the source of his attacks. When depressed, bipolar disorder can result in fearfulness, threats of suicide and depressed mood that can last for hours and even days. If depression and mania occur together that can alternate rapidly over a course of a few days.

There were times when Franklin would stay in bed all day when depressed. Somehow, he always managed to hold a job so he would get up for work and perform well, deepening my confusion and making me feel like functioning for the family was not a priority or desire for him. Other behaviors Franklin demonstrated included extreme fear and nervousness, and a restlessness where he would stay up all night working on a project. He would become very talkative at times, telling stories mostly from his childhood, and he would often have thoughts of death. Sometimes it seemed he would make things up and accuse me of things I did not do but I did not know what delusions were at the time. They were also scary because he was so convincing when he told his stories that it was clear he truly believed what he was saying so it was no surprise that others believed him too. Often, he was the victim in those stories so others would not only believe him but also feel sorry for him while making me the villain. Later, he would deny he ever said or did what he did, but he usually left behind proof in letters.

Treatment for bipolar disorder is typically medications, therapy and sometimes ECT. While in the Air Force, Franklin went through a long list of anti-depressants and anti-psychotics that did not seem to work well. They would either cause him to sleep too much, extreme dry mouth, and the energy from manic phases were squashed so he felt like a zombie. He stayed on Lithium for the longest period before quitting on more than one occasion. I am proud of him for trying for as long as he did.

15

The Cherry Tree

*"Trust in the Lord with all your heard
and do not lean on your own understanding."*

— PROVERBS 3:5 —

We decided to take a family vacation and visit Franklin's parents in Indianapolis, IN and I felt it was necessary to share the diagnosis with his family, at least with his father. It was always difficult for me to spend time with Franklin's family as I was always aware of and reminded that his mother hated me, and I still don't know why. His father and all of his siblings, except for one, were always friendly so I strategically attempted to stay away from my mother-in-law during these visits. Our children always enjoyed the visit with their cousins, many close in age, but my mother-in-law even showed bias against a couple of them, so I was always seeking to protect them as well. There were times when Carole and Charles felt like they were treated differently. I did not see it, so I was not sure if it was intentional or not.

I decided to share Franklin's diagnosis with his father. I figured if anyone would understand what I am going through, certainly he would. He has been married to Franklin's mother for more than 30 years so certainly he has some words of wisdom for me, and I prayed that he could help me understand what I was dealing with. We were sitting in the kitchen, and I said:

"Reverend Hendricks, I have something to tell you".

"What is it?" he asked.

"Franklin has been having some difficulty at work. We went to the hospital for a few evaluations, and they believe he has bipolar disorder."

Reverend Hendricks didn't say a word. He sat there staring in the distance and then abruptly bit down on his pipe with his dentures making a loud chomping sound. He looked at me in silence, but I could tell he didn't know what to say but I could see the pain in his eyes.

Your oldest son is supposed to be your namesake and your future. The reality of an uncertain future had to be hard for him to hear. But this was new for me, and I wish he had shared some words of wisdom with me about what to do because I didn't know what was coming. Like me, he didn't sign up for the genetic disaster of a serious mental illness that has now infiltrated my family. Both of us had plenty of relatives to compare the future with but at this point I just wasn't paying attention. I never thought it would happen in my house. Although, both of us also loved our spouses and entered a covenant before God to love until death do us part.

Reverend Hendricks reluctantly told me that his wife was dealing with Schizophrenia. She had seen a doctor and received a prescription, but he was not able to get her to stay in treatment, so her unpredictable behaviors were a constant source of stress. Schizophrenia is also a brain disorder that can be difficult to understand. It is typically associated with hallucinations, delusions, paranoia, and disorganized thinking.

Schizophrenia seems to be more disruptive to functioning than bipolar and for Mrs. Hendricks that dysfunction was visible in my high school, although we didn't know what it was. When she started having difficulty performing her teaching duties, her family moved her to Chatom and her bizarre behavior came with her. At times she was mean, her lessons were sometimes disorganized, and she definitely seemed to hate me and look at me with suspicion.

As a first lady, there is a lot of responsibility within the church and I feel for my father-in-law who had to cover up or perhaps apologize for some of her behavior. People with schizophrenia typically have a hard time forming bonds with others and as a first lady, a key role is fellowship with parishioners. That expectation started deteriorating over the years to the point of her visible absence in the leadership at the church. Reverend Hendricks watched helplessly as her entire demeanor and personality changed before his eyes.

Stigma still exist, even in families dealing with serious mental illness, and often they will do what they can to hide the reality from the world. Within the church is no exception. Stigma in the church may even be worse because many associate mental illnesses with sin or having an evil spirit. Some churches even tell people with mental illnesses not to take anti-depressants or anti-psychotics even though they are not doctors. They are playing a dangerous game with that advice. If they don't give the same advice to those with diabetes about insulin or those with cancer about chemo or radiation, then they should keep their medical advice about mental illness to themselves as well. Shouldn't all illnesses be seen as rooted in a spirit? Certainly, all illness can be healed from Christ, if it is His will.

I think my father in law really appreciated having someone to talk to. He had kept so much to himself that actually sharing my experience about Franklin seemed to open a door for him to share stories about Mrs. Hendricks with me as well.

"Do you remember when I sent you and Jr. to South Dakota?" he asked.

"Yes, before we left Albuquerque?" I replied wondering where this was going.

"Yes, well there was a lot more to the story," he paused as he seemed pained to talk about this. "I had a strange and surprising conversation with Frances as we sat under a cherry tree in the yard of our home late one evening." he said as he started describing the story.

"Can one make you marry them?" Frances asked.

"No," he told her.

"Are you sure?"

"Yes, I am sure", Reverend Hendricks responded.

"Supposed they kidnap you and force you to marry them?" Mrs. Hendricks asked.

"You would have to agree to a marriage.", he assured her.

"There is a peculiar situation in the community where I live. All are White and they have accepted me as White. There is a certain society there who seek to get certain people married," she said.

"What do you mean?" Reverend Hendricks asked but confused about what she was saying.

"I mean like I am tops in the Education field where I work and this society knows it, and there is a man there in the area that is tops in authority of the government. He is high-up in this respect, but I am high-up in education and this society feels like the two together would bring up the standard," she said.

"Is it the society's idea or is it yours and the man?" Reverend Hendricks asked while becoming increasingly concerned about the conversation.

"Honey", she said, "the society, not me."

"How can this society marry you off when you are already married?", he asked audibly distressed by her words.

"You can go to Mexico and do it, or there is a place out there in Indian Territory where it can be done", she said as she seemed to believe what she was saying.

"It is not legal without a divorce," Reverend Hendricks explained.

"Yes, it is," she insisted.

"That is not so, it is adultery in America," he told her. "What can a person do to you if you promise to marry him and don't do it?"

"He can kill you", she said with fear in her eyes.

"Oh honey, you scare me, you scare me!" Reverend Hendricks exclaimed.

"I did not say they would, I said they could, that depends on how far you have gone."

"You know, Frances, we married November 13 and this year we will have been married 39 years, we have five children, and 22 grand-children. Why didn't you have this desire to marry someone else before?" Reverend Hendricks asked.

"I am accepted as White now."

"So that's your reason?" he asked.

"I have a chance to get up in power and money, she added.

"We are already doing well financially, and we get rent every month, isn't that big money? Are you really losing your mind? Will you throw down 39 years of marriage, honors, 5 children, and 22 grandchildren to do wrong. You have no grounds whatsoever for a divorce. We have lived together peacefully for 39 years. We agreed when we married that I would not interfere with your teaching, and you would not interfere with my preaching. The change in you came since February. We have always lived apart during school terms, but we were together four months out of every year and made frequent visits during the other times, and before you went out there the entire family was here for seven years and since you have been out there you have been coming home, and I hold a letter written by you in February saying you may come home and look after me. Something strange happened since February", Reverend Hendricks scolded her.

"Why did you stop writing or calling me?", he asked.

"I am too busy and tired."

"Is that really the reason?"

"Yes."

"Well, I don't think that's a good reason," he said sadly.

"Well, I write an article for a paper that covers three counties; I write from my area. I write Indian story. I sign my name Jack Hendricks, but they all know that it's me," she said.

"There are people who write a whole book but do not neglect to write or call their family", he said. "Let's go back to this marriage. The man that is so high in power in the government, is he married?"

"I don't know."

"You talk foolish! How could a woman get worked-up over a man and don't even know if he is married or not? Well, I guess you know you are married but you both must have gotten together to marry lawful or non-lawful, regardless of who it may hurt," he said shifting in his seat and trying not to get angry. "Well has he got his master's degree?"

"I don't know"

"You already answered this question anyway because you stated that you were the top out there in education and this man was the top in power.

I don't want you to go back up there", he told her.

"I am going!", she argued.

"Suppose your husband insists that you don't go?"

"I am going at all costs. I am expected to get a new rating when I get back. Letters have already been coming in my drawer at the school dealing with how to supervise teachers. That means I am on my way up. There will be a package coming that I must accept. I have been told to take it or leave it."

"You don't suppose your marriage at government expense is in this package? You know you told me that you would rather marry a man than break a promise and get killed, is this in that package?" he asked.

"I can't talk." she cried.

"You sure are a different woman, haven't we been getting along fine for 39 years? He asked.

"Yes."

"Well, what's the matter now?

"Just being away," she said.

"You didn't have to be away, did you?"

"No", she said.

"I don't want you away now," he pleaded.

"I'm going. I have reared my family and now I am on my own."

"So, you don't have any place for me anymore? He asked her.

"You can get another wife, one woman up there told me you will find somebody. They all say I need a new husband. They all say I do as I please, and I do. I got it made with the high-ups. I had that old Principal moved at Manderson. He felt that I had something to do with it. I went to the man with power, and he is crazy about me, and I told him what he was doing", she said.

"Was he doing something to you?" Reverend Hendricks asked.

"Yes, to all of the teachers. The woman supervisor does not know I went to him. He told me he would go the next day and get on him. I told him no not then. So, it was not long before he was gone. He didn't like me,"

"Why didn't he like you?"

"Well, he wants to attend to people's business. He asked me one day where I go on weekends."

"So, what if he did?"

"It's none of his business. He gave that wench the grade I should have had, and he cannot do half as well as I can, but they moved him." He said he could not understand Mrs. Whirlughorse for anything. She used to admire me very much, not so hot now. They got a principal at another school who finished from Tuskegee but cannot do half as well as I," she said.

"So, you and the powers that be will move those under you out if you get married? Reverend Hendricks asked her. Frances did not reply and just sat there quietly, hopefully realizing how crazy this all sounds.

"You say I cannot spend my vacation with you? Reverend Hendricks asked.

"NO!", she yelled in a way that he never heard her yell before.

"You stay away from my job!", she continued to yell.

"It's not the people that don't want me there from what I can see it is you", he said.

"I will never believe the fine people of your community would not want your own husband to visit you, but I do believe it is you and that you have sold yourself out to a high-up and you don't want me around. If you insist that I don't spend my vacation with you then I know you mean business", he added sadly, with anguish.

"You did say if I come up there you would get me a place at Chadron, Nebraska but the cost would be $6 per day, is that were you spend your weekends?"

"Yes, sometimes", she added.

"Why?"

"People are nice there," she answered.

"And what else?"

"They have a Methodist Church there."

"Do you go?" He asked.

"Yes, I may join. Chadron wants some colored people so bad, at least a couple. You mean integrated couple?"

"Yes. They are nice."

"Well, if integration intends to separate families that is bad. I also say that God's judgement will punish the plotters and the wicked. A good name is worth more than riches. The higher you go up the greater you fall", he told her.

"I cannot tell you the name of this so-called powerful executive of the government because she refused to give it to me, but I threatened to make it public knowledge if she didn't come home," he confided in Virginia.

"That is why I sent Franklin there to talk to her and help convince her to come home when you all were living in Albuquerque. When she came home, we went to see a doctor and they sent her to a psychiatrist who said she had schizophrenia. They gave her medication, but she refused to take it after a couple of days," he told me.

16

A Family Affair

> *"Keeping steadfast love for thousands, forgiving iniquity and transgression and sin, but who will by no means clear the guilty, visiting the iniquity of the fathers on the children and the children's children, to the third and the fourth generation."*
>
> — EXODUS 34:7 —

It was heartbreaking to hear Reverend Hendricks share his story, but it was nice to have that quality time with him. I knew he is probably the only person who could understand what I was going through and what was ahead for me and our family. I was able to talk to him about what I had learned so far about delusions and it seemed from that story that my mother-in-law was full of delusions, disorganized thoughts, possibly inflated self-esteem and I wonder about hallucinations. At the time when the story occurred, he didn't know anything about schizophrenia, but in hindsight it all seemed to make sense to him now that she was diagnosed.

Other stories he shared that day were about incidents of my mother-in-law running down the street naked on more than one occasion. The neighbors and the local police were aware of her bizarre behavior. She was known for being disruptive in the church and the community.

Being a caregiver for a person with mental illness is basically a job. It can be frustrating, embarrassing, confusing, and tiring. It can also be very lonely. If you care for someone with a physical illness, the sympathy and support systems are there to help with meals, fellowship, respite, errands, and more. When you care for someone with a mental illness, people often don't understand, don't know what to say, they are scared, and eventually they avoid you all together.

My mother-in-law refused treatment almost instantly. Franklin resisted it for a while as well, but he did eventually try a lot of different treatment options thanks to the military. Treatment compliance is one of the greatest challenges for caregivers to deal with which is why so many feel like they are always walking on eggshells waiting for the next crisis.

Talking about mental illness with Franklin was so difficult. I never knew what to ask but no matter what I said, he would get defensive and angry. He automatically seemed to think I was trying to take over and strip him of his independence which is so not true. *If* I can't talk to him about it and I can't talk to his doctors about it unless they call me with a threat, what am I to do? Overall, I felt like I was alone other than my father-in-law and I was thankful for him but didn't want to burden him since he had his hands full with a congregation, a district, and basically running the home now as well as cooking and cleaning for his wife.

I was able to see the pain that the news of his eldest son's condition caused him. He knew what my future, as Franklin's wife would bring. He also knew how hard it is to try and ignore mental health. Stigma is strong, especially in the Black community and in the faith community, so as a Presiding Elder in the AME-Zion church I can only imagine what he was dealing with on a regular basis. People can accept physical illness for every organ in the body, except the brain. It is as if a concerted effort has occurred to pretend like those impacted by mental illness are pretending or that it was a direct result of sin. Was the bible a contributor to this? After all David did fake mental illness and yet acknowledged his depression and struggle with despair. Many churches preach against mental health treatment and a general belief in society is that mental illness is a result of sin and punishment from God. The result is suffering in silence and isolation.

We got up the next morning and got ready for church. We were going to Penick Chapel and Reverend Hendricks was preaching. Getting five kids ready for church is always a chore, so of course we walk in late while the choir is singing and have to go all the way to the front as the guest of the pastor and first lady. I watch as my father-in-law slowly walks to the pulpit. I couldn't help but remember our discussion last night and I felt the pain in his heart as he began to speak.

"I want to preach to you today on the subject "Jesus has the cure for a sick and ailing world. The Word today comes from II Kings 5:10 and 1 John 1:7.

This indeed is a sick age. It is sick in so many ways. Sick body, sick mind, and sick soul. When we visit hospitals and see the mass of people there we say, there are plenty of sick people, that's true but what you see there is not the beginning of the people that are sick. They are sick in homes, in the streets, and on the job. And the same can be said about those that are sick in the mind.

I do not know which sickness is worse to us, the sickness of the body or the sickness of the mind. The mind is the worse, I believe but both are bad. And then comes the sickness of the soul and heart. But if we can get the heart and soul healed then the whole man will be alright, and Jesus has the cure for an ailing world."

I wasn't sure where he was going with this opening, and I could see both Franklin and his mother squirm a little in their seats. But he continued down the heart and soul path, rebuking greed and worldly things and the healing power of God. After service, we joined the parishioners for a meal in fellowship hall so everyone could greet and catch up with us since it had been a while since Franklin, Jr. had attended church service.

I realized there was so much more I just didn't know about Franklin and his family. I still knew nothing about bi-polar disorder or any other mental health conditions. I didn't know what to do to even get the information and if I had it what could I do? I felt utterly helpless and afraid. Since I did not fully understand the big picture, it would be years before I realized the heredity factors that could affect our children.

Reverend Hendricks and I knew by now that this was a family affair and both of us were committed to our spouses. Franklin's mother had a sister with schizophrenia who was institutionalized in a psychiatric facility after chasing her twin sons around with a butcher knife. Mind you, this was after five of her fifteen children mysteriously died before the age of one. What is it about knives and schizophrenia in this family? He also had a first cousin with schizophrenia who was believed to have killed her lesbian lover and somehow avoided jail time. Another cousin, with bipolar disorder, was doing well academically and seemed to be able to work successfully as a college professor but he was clearly socially awkward, and some described him as creepy. Their family was well educated but knew how to cover things up and then in return they would pretend like nothing happened due to shame and stigma that interfered with folks obtaining proper help. You know how stigma works, you use other descriptions and there are plenty of examples of unexplained "hospitalizations for many years before death," or "unemployed due to disability," or perhaps those adults who never launched and continued to live at home with their parents. Of course, we will never know the full story regarding those who are self-medicating with alcohol or other substances. There are rumors of alcoholism and some of those cousins died at very young ages. Regardless, the reality of what these families were dealing with, like me and my father-in-law, just were not openly discussed. If it had been discussed, I have no doubt different decisions would have been made and perhaps some of the tragic endings could have been avoided. I really needed some advice at that moment, but I quickly saw I would get no advice from my father-in-law, at least not right now. I know it is not because he did not want to help me, I know he was now grieving his son and likely did not know what to tell me because he had struggles of his own.

Once I was finally able to talk to one of Franklin's psychiatrist, he assured me that bi-polar would not likely be diagnosed with our children but possibly our grandchildren. However, because Franklin's mother had a diagnosis of schizophrenia, our children could possibly have some type of serious mental illness in their future.

The diagnosis of bipolar was hard for Franklin to hear as well. He immediately felt his future was bleak. He couldn't see a possibility of a "normal" life. At one point, Franklin tried to insist that I leave him and take the children because he "wasn't going to be any good." This would be the most difficult time of our life so far and I had great fear of the unknown ahead. I loved Franklin with all my heart, and I could not imagine a life without him.

The next two years would bring three more sources of grief in my life, the loss of a child, the hint of mental illness with another child resulting in another leaving our family. The grief and fear were trying to destroy my spirit and threatening my family. "God give me strength" was my constant prayer.

My oldest son, Charles, was born at home by Cousin Joan. The delivery was hard, and the use of obstetrical forceps was used and resulted in his head being deformed. I believe they also resulted in causing epilepsy and hearing loss for Charles. Despite that, Charles was very smart, kind, and never caused us any problems. He did his chores, performed well in school, and was loved by all except Lyle who couldn't seem to get along with any of his siblings.

Lyle was a bully who called other people names and often called Charles stupid. Lyle would often get kicked out of school for causing problems with teachers and he truly seemed to believe he knew more than everyone else even though he was a child. He had a lot of unexplained anger and rage, and he even took that out on our dogs. He found pleasure in upsetting his siblings and always seemed to look for buttons to push to start a fight. I didn't know that these could be symptoms of bipolar disorder in a child.

One day when my uncle Cecil and his wife Joyce were visiting, Lyle overheard her talking about Charles's biological father, my first husband, Joshua Taylor. Of course, Lyle couldn't wait to run and tell Charles that he wasn't his real brother. Charles was still in high school and after I shared the details of his father and how Franklin adopted him as an infant, Charles didn't know what to think or do. It was very emotional, and I was guilt ridden for having not told him before, but we thought it would be best not to tell him that. Lyle finding pleasure in destroying the spirit of his brother was a clear indication that something was not right with this boy beyond just being mean. Charles would decide to finish high school in Alabama to get to know his biological father, but he would live with my mother and three younger sisters who were still at home.

My fourth source of grief during these two years would be when I became pregnant again. I already had five children and my doctors were afraid for my safety this time. I had an IUD that was lost in my uterus, I had passed out a few times and the doctors suggested abortion due to health fears and stress overload. The military arranged for a private facility to terminate the pregnancy against Franklin's will. He had to sign for the abortion and reluctantly he did after the doctors expressed fears that I wouldn't survive the delivery. I was so sick and unable to function as a wife or mother during the early weeks of the pregnancy, but my health was restored after the abortion. This added to my stress and Franklin's depression during the worst two years of my life where I sought spiritual guidance, prayer and support, which did offer some relief.

17

Military Transition

"And the Lord spoke to Moses, saying, "This applies to the Levites: from twenty-five years old and upward they shall come to do duty in the service of the tent of meeting. And from the age of fifty years they shall withdraw from the duty of the service and serve no more. They minister to their brothers in the tent of meeting by keeping guard, but they shall do no service. Thus, shall you do to the Levites in assigning their duties."

— Numbers 8:23-26 —

Franklin had always planned to retire with 20 years of service, but as his mental illness worsened it interfered with his duties, and hospitalizations were increasing. While at Andrews Air Force Base, Washington, DC, he was experiencing severe back pain that was labeled psychosomatic. He spent almost a year in the hospital and by March the doctor had basically given up on Franklin and plans were underway for a medical discharge from the Air Force.

Franklin went to Indianapolis to see if he could get a job but was discouraged and decided he needed more time before retiring. I know he was afraid of civilian life and concerned that he wouldn't make it outside of the Air Force. I suspect that is a common concern for many retiring service members, but I guess his depression, anxiety, and heavy medications, made this transition possibility even harder to grasp.

Because of the Franklins health, the Air Force only agreed to extend Franklin's military service if he would agree to continue treatment. I feel like he became a test subject at this point. Additional medications and treatments did buy Franklin another year or two in the Air Force and a different retirement location, still not too far from his parents.

In the military when you refuse assignments you eventually must choose between a military discharge or to accept a job you don't like so Franklin agreed to go to the island of Guam. Franklin's assignment in Guam was different than any other. This was a strategic air command (SAC) base where he supervised bomb loaders on B52's going to Vietnam.

The kids and I enjoyed the beach, and in Guam I was involved in the Yigo General Baptist Church and really enjoyed working with the youth programs. Guam is an island in the Pacific Ocean so surfing was popular as the waves were amazing. The schools were off post, so the kids attended public schools along with the native Guamanians for the first time in their lives. They often came home talking about kids getting into fights and occasionally stabbed in the parking lots. Carole complained of being bullied for being fat and quiet. Belinda experienced a racial slur for the first time in her life in the elementary school from a boy who lived next door to us on the military base. Her older brothers, Lester and Charles, told her what to say back to him but that was not such a good idea as she ended up being threatened to have her mouth washed out with the same bar of soap, they used on the neighbor kid. Charles was getting settled in at Chatom High back home with Muh and I missed him dearly.

The military personnel on Guam were living in tents and Franklin was dealing with multiple psychiatric issues among his team members. The stress of this assignment was just too much for Franklin as well and he ended up being admitted to a psychiatric unit there on the island for his own mental health. This time, instead of numbness in his leg, he was experiencing severe back pain. He was treated with aspirin and Darvon. After discharge, he also used the valium I had left. When that ran out, he returned to the doctor and was given Elavil. Nothing seemed to help. He started demonstrating some paranoia and believed the other employees were harassing him. It got so bad with a couple of his female coworkers that he admitted to becoming homicidal and suicidal and his depression increased. He was agitated, his speech was not clear and sometimes incoherent, and he was fixated on death.

Eventually the doctor decided to return him to the states for additional psychiatric treatment and to begin the process for a medical discharge. Franklin was transferred to Wright Patterson AFB where he would remain for two months. The kids and I remained in Guam for a couple more months so the kids could finish the school year before joining him in Ohio. We were in Guam for less than a year.

Franklin wasn't home a month before he became suicidal again. It was odd because he was functional at work and performed well but once he got home, he would stay in his room, and he just couldn't seem to get it together. He often thought about rejoining his Uncle Ike and Aunt Lydia and fantasized about dying so he could talk to them. He also told his doctors about multiple affairs for 15 years of his marriage and didn't know how to tell me. Not confessing was leading to increased guilt, depression and again he became suicidal.

Franklin was admitted to the hospital again after having suicidal ideations of driving his car into a truck with his two sons, Lyle and

Lester, in the car. He thought death would be pleasant and his pain would go away. Before this admission he was having night terrors from dreams about death, usually around two or three in the morning. His anxiety continued to contribute to neck and back pain and eventually headaches. New medications like Thorazine were added to the existing prescription of Elavil. Nothing was working.

On top of everything else, Franklin was experiencing stress from worry about his parent's health, a large knot on his mother's neck, hypertension of his father, and the closing of our house in Ohio. As he continued to struggle to cope, he was admitted to the hospital again, and a military medical discharge was underway.

"Ready or not, my twenty-two-year career with the Air Force is ending," Franklin said. "The Air Force is all I have known as an adult. It is all I have ever wanted to do since I was a teenager. It cost me a lot to get in and now I feel lost leaving on a forced medical retirement with just a GED and little transferrable skills from my military service."

I stayed quiet, not sure how to respond and feeling a little scared myself. This is all I had known in my adult life as well. Although I was working in a grocery store at that moment, the rest of my twenty years with Franklin had been spent raising our five kids. I had only been working less than five years and certainly did not consider this job a career.

I wanted so much more for myself, but we had to figure out how to care for our family and cover our bills on the significantly reduced retirement salary that was coming. We were only 39 years old! Since his pending discharge was based on mental illness, we didn't know what kind of job he was even going to be able to get. If he wasn't able to work, I was worried about what I could do to increase our household income enough to care for the kids.

It was a very stressful season. We had two kids still in high school, one in junior high, and one still in elementary. The older they were getting the more expensive food, clothes, cars, insurance, college, and who knows what else was going to cost. I was trying not to show my fear to Franklin who right then needed some encouragement and not to hear about my worries and fears which would for all I know send him into another suicidal crisis.

"Well Franklin, I have faith that a good job option will work out for you. Is the Air Force helping you with that?" I asked hoping not to stir up negative emotions in him.

"They are offering suggestions and referring us to the VA. I think I am going to apply at the post office and then look at options for going back to school," he said with hope and expectation.

"You know, I could go back to school as well," I said with hesitation "I have been thinking about being a dental hygienist," I mumbled as I expected resistance.

"I think the kids and I need you here," he said with more gentleness, understanding, awareness than I had expected. "If we are both working and going to school, who will be here to take care of the house and have dinner ready?"

Biting my tongue and holding back the tears, I stayed quiet not wanting to start a fight. I feel so hopeless that this is all my life holds for me, yet I want so much more. I want so much more for my girls as well. I pray they will never be this dependent on a man for anything. I am praying for my perseverance and strength to remain committed to my marriage.

Franklin left the Air Force after 22 years of service with a GED he obtained while on active duty. We both started taking a few basic college classes in Guam and we both wanted more but only he would go on to pursue his education at this time. I really enjoy learning and I made the most of these rare opportunities but still felt cheated from having a career of my own.

Franklin's first job after his military discharge was at the US Postal Service. He worked at night as a letter sorting machine operator so that he could attend classes during the day. Since he worked at night he would come home and sleep most of the day so neither me nor the kids really saw him much. I would leave for work as he was coming in from work and the kids would be in school. This continued for about six years.

18

Baptism of the Holy Spirit

We attended the spiritual conference sponsored by the Air Force one fall in Ridgecrest, North Carolina. Ridgecrest is just outside of Asheville and primarily known for their Christian Conference Center in the beautiful Blue Ridge Mountains. We arrived at Ridgecrest Baptist Campus early afternoon and attended the night services. It was a beautiful spirit filled night of praise and worship.

The following morning, we attended the devotion service, a parent education training session, and bible study. After these sessions, they had a group session conducted by Air Force chaplains and Franklin chose the spiritual growth session. During the first class, participants gave individual testimonies, and time went by so fast that the group decided to meet again the same day at a time which would not conflict with the regularly scheduled program.

At our next impromptu session, over fifty people showed up along with Baptist, Methodist, and Pentecostal ministers. We sang praises to God, prayed, and several others gave their testimonies. In the midst of one prayer, a minister came over to Franklin and told him he could receive the Baptism of the Holy Spirit right then if he wanted to. Our whole purpose of traveling to this conference was so that Franklin could seek whatever he could receive from God so of course he agreed and welcomed the laying of hands. Franklin received the fullness of God's spirit and believed he was healed. He immediately started speaking in tongues. Because of his faith that he was healed, he stopped taking medication for his back pain and depression that day and continued to Praise the Lord in his talk and his walk.

19

Death and Loss

For everything there is a season, and a time for every matter under heaven: a time to be born, and a time to die; a time to plant, and a time to pluck up what is planted; a time to kill, and a time to heal; a time to break down, and a time to build up; a time to weep, and a time to laugh; a time to mourn, and a time to dance; a time to cast away stones, and a time to gather stones together; a time to embrace, and a time to refrain from embracing; a time to seek, and a time to lose; a time to keep, and a time to cast away; a time to tear, and a time to sew; a time to keep silence, and a time to speak; a time to love, and a time to hate; a time for war, and a time for peace.

— ECCLESIASTES 3:1-8 —

Just as Franklin retires from the Air Force, moving to Ohio to be closer to his family in Indiana, he is cheated of the opportunity to enjoy his parents. An old-wives tale speaks of how all of us have three

95

simultaneous major deaths in our life. Although Uncle Josiah was the first traumatic loss for Franklin followed by his Aunt Lucy, there would be three additional deaths, one that would not only cause major trauma and complicated grief for him but would also haunt our family for years to come.

The phone rang in the middle of the night and it was Franklin's sister screaming in the phone

"Daddy is dead! Daddy is dead!"

Franklin was silent and just held the phone as he began to sob. I took the phone but could not get Charlotte to calm down and the story was sketchy. I heard knife, blood, bathtub. Over the next few days, we would learn that it was just his father and my mother-in-law at home that night. All the doors were not just locked but they were double locked. All the windows were locked as well. Reverend Hendricks was fully clothed around 11pm at night and his dentures were in place, which is unusual for him. Even more strange was the suitcase that was packed, a roll of cash in his pocket, and he was found lying in a pool of his own blood inside the home's bathtub.

The knife, believed to be the weapon, was found under the mattress of the couple's bed. Apparently, she had removed the knife from her husband's chest, while he was in the bathtub, and took it to her bedroom and placed it under a mattress. The story they would tell the detectives is that Reverend Hendricks committed suicide. Franklin and I both had a hard time believing that story. Unfortunately, the alternative would be arresting his wife who had schizophrenia and sending her to jail in her now mentally fragile state.

A prominent preacher's wife couldn't have possibly done this and no one in the community knew she had schizophrenia. So, to spare the family, the police did not arrest her or charge her, but God would. Many family members continue to refuse to acknowledge what happened that night. The denial of mental illness is so strong in this family, and they can't even acknowledge that their mother had schizophrenia, in spite of the medical diagnosis, shock treatments she received, the meds she refused to take and the escalating paranoid and bizarre behavior for many years that continued until she took the life of her husband of almost 50 years, Reverend Hendricks.

The night we heard of this tragedy, Franklin prepared to leave early the next morning, but I would have to wait and join him with the kids. The girls were just 10 and 13. Charles was in Alabama, Lyle was at Ohio State, and Lester was a senior in High School getting ready to go to Tennessee State. When the girls and I arrived in Indianapolis, the house was quieter than I had ever remembered. To my surprise my mother-in-law was sitting at the table quietly. No one knew what to say to her, so everyone sat in silence. Suddenly, she looked up from the table and said slowly, clearly and shockingly:

"And he thought he was going to leave me".

I was speechless and developed a pain in the pit of my stomach. Did she just admit to murdering Reverend Hendricks? No one else was here so who would believe me. I decided to keep quiet until I spoke to Franklin privately.

As we spoke to the detectives it appeared that for him to have committed suicide, he would have had to place the knife to his heart and run into the wall so hard that it would pierce his heart. So how could this have happened in a bathtub? We could tell the detectives did not believe that, but the police decided not to arrest her. After all it was a domestic dispute, she was now a widow, and their five children were insisting that there was no way their mother could have killed their father. Who would think such a thing? A Presiding Elder in charge of all the local AME churches in the state, a man with political influence, a large social network, and loved by all who knew him. How could his wife of 40 years possibly find it in her heart to stab him to death? No one, including me, wanted to believe that. Suicide would be listed on the death certificate. Their children agree and yet for me that was more of a disservice and a disgrace for a preacher's legacy.

My feelings about this are not because my mother-in-law didn't treat me well, not because most who knew her saw her as mean and arrogant, not because she treated my children different than her other grandchildren, but how could they taint the legacy of this great man of God who was loved by all, including me? It just didn't seem fair. I guess if it were my mom, maybe just maybe, I would look at it differently, but I guess I just think the truth should prevail no matter what. By putting that label of suicide down on that paper, there was no further investigation warranted by the detectives. The case was closed.

I can't help but recall Reverend Hendricks's sermon from years ago on perseverance and yet it comforted me in knowing that he was now in a better place. He persevered years of verbal abuse. He was not only a Presiding Elder, but he was the caretaker, often doing all of the cooking and caring for the kids the best he could. He was also devastated by the diagnosis of his son who would continue to be challenged by the genetic inheritance of the Cunningham family. What a heartbreak to have known that his eldest son would also have a damaged quality of life because of genetics and a rebellion to the total ways of God. He was to follow a long line of preachers who came before his father and he chose to run off to the military, without their permission at the age of 17. As Reverend Hendricks stated so many years ago in his sermon *Perseverance: It's Price and Its Profit*: "I have run the great race, I have finished the course, I have kept the faith…" That was the price. Then Paul mentions the profit of his perseverance: "And now the prize awaits me, the garland of righteousness which God awards me…"

Franklin has never dealt with grief and loss very well. The last two deaths in his family, his Uncle Josiah and his Aunt Lucy were very hard for him to get over and he would end up in deep depressions and almost suicidal. This was no different. He spent many nights crying and many days sleeping in a dark room. When he is depressed, there is no reasoning, no encouraging that works.

Amazingly, he was still able to function on his job just not socially or with his family. He was the oldest in the family, so they relied on him to take care of business. He did have help and support from his siblings, and they discussed options for their mother and agreed to all do their part to help her after this tragedy. Franklin was able to hold it together to get through the funeral and multiple celebrations of life that followed.

Choir intro: We've come this far by faith, leaning on the Lord. Trusting in His holy name. He never failed us yet. Ohh oh oh oh oh, can't turn around, we've come this far by faith. I will trust in the Lord; I will trust in the Lord. I will trust in the Lord, til I die. I will trust in the Lord, I will trust in the Lord, I will trust in the Lord, til I die.

Bishop Hoggard approached the podium.

Members of the bereaved family, ministers, members, and friends. We the ministers and officers of the Indiana Conference have come here today to express our respect and deepest sympathy to the bereaved family and friends of our brother, Reverend Franklin Hendricks, Sr. who has crossed the bar.

We can only say of him that he had a dream to build a Tabernacle unto the Lord for Zion that all who worship therein might hear the Word of God. Rest assured his life was not in vein and we will work together to finish the work that he started. In this work he had the course of a Joshua with the ability to hold on to the task until it was finished no matter how hard or how tough.

O it is hard to work for God,
To rise and take his part
Upon this battlefield of earth
And not sometimes lose heart!

He hides himself so wondrously,
As though there was no God
He is least seen when all the powers
of ill are most abroad;

Or he deserts us in the hour
The fight is all but lost;
And seems to leave us to ourselves
Just when we need him most.

It is not so, but so it looks;
And we lose courage then;
And doubts will come if God hath kept
His promises to men.

To the family, we commend you to our Heavenly Father who does
everything well and who is too wise to error. Our dear brother ran the race
well. To live a Christian life is the best life one can live and he truly loved
the church through the good and the bade and he was faithful to the end.
I will close with the words of John Ellerton:

Now, the laborer's task is over;
Now, the battle day is past;
Now, upon the farthest shore
Lands the voyager at last

Father, in thy gracious keeping
Leave we now, thy servant sleeping.

There the tears of earth are dried;
There the hidden things are clear
There the work of list is tried,
By a juster judge than here.

Father, in thy gracious keeping
Leave thee now, thy servant sleeping.

(One of Reverend Hendricks's favorite songs "A Charge to keep I Have" started playing softly in the background and as he finished speaking the choir started to sing as our niece approached the podium to recite a poem)

"To be able to smile in the storm
To be watchful and careful in prayer
To be cautious to do no one harm
To be useful and wanting to live everyday
That whenever the bell tolls for him
He'll be happy to say my end is at hand
I have done all the good I could do"

One by one for what seemed to be hours, family, friends, and church members, stepped up to give their tributes to my father-in-law. And finally, the service closed, the meal in the basement completed, and it was off to the home of Paul and Frances to have final greetings from those closest to the family. What a physically and emotional day for us all.

I always saw Mrs. Hendricks as mean and bougie but I did not know she had been diagnosed with schizophrenia until a few years before my father-in-law died. Like I said, people didn't talk about mental health and certainly did not admit to problems. I think it is hard enough being Black in America but to add a serious mental illness like bipolar or schizophrenia must be viewed as unbearable to many, especially for a first lady of an AME Zion district. Unfortunately, the cover up is not the answer either. To act like things don't exist doesn't make it so and this family apparently has been efficient at covering things up. To let my father-in-law, have suicide added to his death certificate instead of the reality of murder because of schizophrenia was just too much for this family to face.

Although Mrs. Hendricks's eyes have always had a strange, almost evil glare that could cause nightmares for at least one of my children, looking at Mrs. Hendricks now was like looking at a shell of a woman that was my high school teacher so many years ago. I can't tell if she is there or if a soul even exists in her anymore. She was not the same person and I felt in my soul that the woman I have known all these years was gone.

First lady Hendricks would never recover from the act of evil of taking the life of Reverend Hendricks. She would never act or speak like herself again after that night. She became totally dependent on others for her personal care including bathing. She would eat on command but her thoughts and functioning or decision, making were gone. It was a very sad situation to watch. No matter how much she hurt me over the years, I genuinely felt compassion and love for her at that moment. I would never wish this on anyone.

Her five children decided to take turns caring for her a few months at a time. Knowing that she has hated me all my life, this was a true test of love. I can recall another sermon from my father-in-law on the "3 I am's of Paul" where he stated, "it is an act of grace of the spirit of Christ to feel indebted to the enemy." Despite my husband's health challenges, I am indebted to my mother-in-law for producing him and he has been a great husband and father for over 20 years. I will do whatever I can to support my husband through this crisis with his mother.

Our youngest daughter, now 12, was sometimes asked to help watch her grandmother after school and at times would help her with her baths which sometimes meant physically getting in the shower to help her wash. I know that was hard for her and I am sure it among other life experiences contributed to her career choice of Social Work.

After a couple of years, Mrs. Hendricks deteriorated to the point of requiring a nursing home. This was very hard on Franklin who asked that he never be admitted to a nursing home. The smell in those places was never nice and watching his mother deteriorate to nothing could not have been easy for him. She went from an almost 300 pound 5'8" woman to just under 100 pounds when she died. It was if her life was literally sucked out of her slowly and disastrously. Towards the end of her life, Franklin and I went to visit frequently. He continued to pray for her, and her death would be just one more loss for him that would also change his life. I can't help but wonder if her horrible death was simply punishment for taking the life of one of God's elders in the church. Sin does not exempt us from punishment when we fail to seek forgiveness.

The last month of her life she was no longer able to speak. She could look at you and she would squeeze your hand when speaking. Once when we were alone, I decided to ask her directly about the death of her husband. I asked, "Did you kill Reverend Hendricks?" She glared at me and then gently squeezed my hand. That was confirmation for me. To top that off, I heard Franklin praying that God give him a sign and specifically, he asked that she die on the same date of the month as his father if indeed she did kill his father. She died in her sleep on the 25th of April; Reverend Hendricks was murdered on the 25th of February a few years earlier.

I do believe in forgiveness. I do believe that God forgives us of our sins. I pray that Mrs. Hendricks was able to seek that forgiveness for herself before her death. However, I can't help but think about God's grace and know that since she had a brain disorder that altered her thinking, wouldn't her death bring about complete healing and restoration and her new life as a Christian in her youth would still bring about her salvation in her death? So perhaps she is joined in heaven as a new angel in glory fully restored of her right mind and health for her body. That is much more peaceful of a thought than the alternative and we shall understand it later by and by.

Franklin was named the executor of the estate for his parents after his mother died. The will instructed him to divide all assets evenly between the five children. Franklin's next heartbreak would come when his two youngest sisters decided to dispute the will and file a lawsuit against Franklin because they believed they were entitled to more that their 20% of the estate. Although the case was settled in favor of the original will, this would cause a great deal of stress and depression for Franklin as he felt betrayed. Grief affects everyone differently. When you have a biologically based brain disorder, grief can be complicated. The weight of grief and loss can be so heavy that it triggers symptoms of bipolar disorder. Having a strong support system during a time of loss is extra important for Franklin. Being attacked by his sisters after the loss of their parents just made his recovery from that grief state even harder. A few years later his third loss would come.

The third traumatic loss for Franklin was the death of his brother, Jerome, just over 10 years later. Jerome was his only brother and much loved. Jerome was a good-hearted free spirit who like to have a good time. Jerome was a motorcycle rider and a member of a motorcycle club, and he was away at a club conference when a massive heart attack ended his life instantly. This was yet another traumatic experience for Franklin. He lost his younger brother so suddenly and again the grief process would be very hard on his spirit. We learned about his death from another panic call which came from his sister in Indianapolis.

"Franklin!" Charlotte cried.

"What is it sis?" he asked.

"Jerome is dead", she screamed.

"What?"

She repeated, "Jerome is dead."

And all I could hear and see was tears and Franklin wailing.

"No, no, no, no, not my brother", he sobbed and whimpered and cried out with such pain that my heart was breaking.

He loved his brother deeply and I feared this would be another breaking point for him. Franklin's younger brother collapsed at a biker's club convention from a massive heart attack. I tried to remain calm, but I grew anxious and fearful because I knew that Franklin did not handle grief very well. The grief distracted him, but the loss would push him further down a road of self-destruction.

Every loss in his life, from his uncle who he felt was mistreated, to his father who he believed was murdered by his own mother, to his mother who he believes was punished by God for her sin as we all watched her physically deteriorate before our eyes – all left Franklin with suicidal ideations. He wanted to join his parents and brother in heaven. At least this time he didn't have a plan or actually make an attempt.

His baby brother whom he loved dearly had unexpectedly died in the prime of his life. Often grief can lead a person with bipolar disorder straight into mania. For Franklin, the manic symptoms included not sleeping, staying busy all-night doing things around the house, delusions, being hyperverbal, or going to bars until they closed, and spending money he did not have.

Being the Christian that Franklin was, he was able to restore his relationship with his siblings and they came together to celebrate the life of their brother who was taken too soon.

20

Mid-Life Madness

*"And whatever my eyes desired I did not keep from them.
I kept my heart from no pleasure, for my heart found pleasure
in all my toil, and this was my reward for all my toil. Then
I considered all that my hands had done and the toil I had
expended in doing it, and behold, all was vanity and a striving
after wind, and there was nothing to be gained under the sun."*

— ECCLESIASTES 2:10-11 —

Life soon resumed back to working and raising our kids. Soon, one by one our five kids would all leave home for work, military, or college. Just when I thought we could get back to enjoying the things we love like traveling; our lives began riding a roller coaster that would eventually be the end of our marriage.

Franklin walked in as usual around 5:35 pm kissed me on lips and then went off into the bedroom to get ready for dinner. I

107

followed him today because I wanted him to know I needed to talk to him.

"I have been thinking about going back to school". Franklin didn't respond. "Franklin, did you hear me?"

"Yes, I heard you."

"I want to take some classes at Sinclair College working towards a dental hygienist career." Franklin still did not respond. "Belinda is old enough to fend for herself, and I would go after work."

"So, what about dinner? Franklin asked.

"I can cook extra on the days I am not in class so you will have food to eat when I am not here," I assured him.

His silence made it clear that he was not supportive, but he also did not say no. It is his basic pouting behavior that will come out in other ways later. Although silent, I knew he was going to go do something drastic to show his displeasure. Regardless, I registered for some basic classes at a local community college the next day and could not wait to get started.

I never understood Franklin's resistance to me wanting to have a career for myself. I had been raising our kids all of my adult life and I took very good care of him and our children. The kids were at a point where they did not need me as much, so I saw this as the perfect time to do something for myself. I had supported him through his under-graduate and graduate studies and he now had a career in Social Work. What is wrong with me wanting more for myself? Was it just power and control? Did he just not want me to have anything for myself? I was trying not to resent him for his lack of support, but then I knew I would have to brace myself for his internal and passive aggressive rebellion against my decision.

My time away from home was only a couple nights a week. While I was in class Franklin would find things to get into outside of the home even though if I were there we would just be existing together in the house. Unfortunately, those things he got into involved drinking which lessened his impulse control and thus spending came along with that. Franklin started going out to bars and at times he would buy drinks for everyone in the bar and saw nothing wrong with it. Other times he would find random strangers to give money to.

Over twenty years of sobriety went down the drain. With alcoholism comes many addictive, impulsive, and manipulative behaviors. When you have bipolar disorder, this goes to a whole new level of disaster. The combination of alcohol and lithium can cause even more impaired thinking that already exists for a person with bipolar disorder. The destructive choice of alcohol instead of medication resulted in him going back into symptomatic behavior associated with the condition including anger, sometimes rage, irritability, changes in energy, too little and sometimes too much sleep, and just bizarre behavior. Sometimes I wasn't sure if or when he slept. At other times, I couldn't get him out of the bed unless he had to go to work because he was out of sick leave.

Franklin started staying out until the wee hours of the night. He would come home and listen to music as loud as he could stand, or he would watch TV for the rest of the night. At least the TV was far enough from the bedroom that he wouldn't wake me up. It was like a flashback to the first six years of our marriage and I couldn't help but wonder what he was really doing out there in the streets.

"Franklin, could you turn that down please," I had to yell.

"I like being able to hear it," he would yell back not caring that he was disturbing my sleep.

"I have to get up and go to work in the morning and so do you."

But he continued with his attack on me.

"Why are you always so negative and complaining? I swear it's like living with a probation officer, he grumbled.

I was always "negative and complaining" when he didn't want to hear what I had to say. Nevertheless, he decided to be considerate and turn the music down. The next morning, we drove to work like nothing ever happened and we barely spoke to each other. This was typical pouting behavior as well and the frequency was increasing so I never knew when he would become moody.

The highs and lows of Franklin were continuous and unpredictable, and I continued to walk on eggshells. Delusions of grandeur for him meant thinking that he had a lot of money. His impulse control was the greatest challenge to try and manage during these times as his spending would repeatedly go out of control if I wasn't trying to monitor it.

Although I could see the delusions, he thought everything was perfectly fine. He has always been that kind-hearted person who wanted to help others. He has always been willing to go out of his way to try to "save the world" one person at a time. He would not hesitate to give the shirt off his back if someone asked for it, or if he felt someone was genuinely in need. I actually loved that about him early in our marriage. But now, this was a source of constant fear and anxiety for me because I feared we would end up losing everything, including our home, if he continued down this path of impulsively giving without thinking and driving us deeper and deeper in debt.

Man o' man, if I tried to show Franklin what he was doing and how impulsive his spending decisions were, it would always result in a temper tantrum. His go to response was always to remind me that he made most of the money in our home and that he could do as he pleased. He would often remind me that it was his money he was spending, and he was the man of the house and the man did as he pleased. He seemed to feel that I was trying to control him or dictate his choices. My strategy to distract him from spending was to build a social life. I tried my best to fill our free time with fishing, bowling, and card parties.

Franklin and I loved to fish, and we often took charter or party boats out for a day to deep-sea fish. Eventually we started talking about getting our own boat. We had been looking at several boats at different boat shows one summer both locally and sometimes at Lake Erie in Sandusky, Ohio. We were both interested in the Bayliners brand, so we looked at one particular store several times. Of all the boats we looked at, this brand appealed to us the most. It was literally a home on the water. It had a kitchen, a bedroom, a bathroom with a shower and a full-sized bed.

"Franklin," I would say in knowing that he was impulsive and hoping to get him to take a minute and evaluate the options before us. "Why don't we take all of these brochures and information back home and sit down and review all of the information and review our budget before we make a final decision."

I could see Franklin becoming visibly irritated. He paced a little. Then he paced some more and then he started going side-to-side looking like he was almost dancing. Then he yelled at me saying,

"I work, and I can't buy what I want?I should be able to get what I want if I work for it."

"OK." I said, doing what I always did and surrendering to the battle.

I just couldn't take another fight, another argument with him yelling at me. I found myself becoming more and more afraid of his words and tirades.

"You are right;you can get what you want but don't ask me to sign the loan," I said softly.

Franklin said with belligerence, hostility, and apathy. "You don't have to sign."

Franklin pushed forward to apply for a boat loan but of course, with his free spending and high debt already, the loan officer came back and told him he needed a co-signer. Predictably, like every other time, he pouted until I gave in, and I ended up signing as a co-owner.

Regardless of how he managed to get his way, he was so excited to have a new toy to play with. I guess I was a little too. I knew he couldn't afford it, but I also know this is one thing we could actually do and distract him from other destructive behaviors. We had lots of fun on the boat. We spent lots of weekend relaxing and enjoying ourselves on the open water. Since our last child, Belinda, was in college we were able to go away almost every weekend. It was really nice getting away together or with other couples to fish. It was relaxing and actually some real quality time. Just when it seemed like we were relaxed and enjoying our empty nest life together another impulsive decision came a year later.

About a year after Jerome died, Franklin suddenly and without warning or provocation wanted to move from Ohio all the way to Florida.

Franklin came home one day and said, "Virginia, I have decided we are going to move to Florida!"

"What?" I said bewildered and a bit shocked.

"Why in the world would we do that?" I asked wondering where this was coming from.

What is he thinking now? I was blindsided by this and didn't know what to say.

"Because that is what people do to get ready for retirement. Aren't you tired of these cold winters? We could fish all year in Florida," he said, excited at the prospect of this new idea and being able to fish more often. "I saw a job opening in Orlando and I submitted and application."

He indeed had applied for a transfer to the Orlando VA without even talking to me first, and of course he got it. He would have to report by the first of February. I had no interest in moving to Florida. I have two sisters there and it is nice to visit, but I have never thought about moving there. After traveling with the Air Force all those years, we finally settled in here, I had friends and a job here and now he wants to pick up and move again at this age?

What was I going to do in Florida? It meant leaving a steady job to move to a state I know nothing about with a man who is making impulsive decisions. Our oldest son had moved there but three of our other children were in Ohio and Michigan so I would be further away from them, and all my friends were here in Ohio. I was just starting school to become a dental hygienist so once again, I had to put my interest to the side, be the good wife, and follow my husband's lead. I was tired of continuing in this unpredictable way. I know that I am supposed to honor my husband's wishes but at what point do I get to follow my own. At what point can we have stability and contentment. Will I ever have this. Will we always be jumping from one of his whims to the next?

We were no longer going to church or praying together by then. I was a firm believer that Franklin's faith kept him healthy, sober, and in remission from bipolar and alcoholism. He was still and always would be a Christian, he knew the Word; he had led probably close to forty individuals to follow Jesus Christ during his earlier outreach. I had no doubt about his future in eternity with God. I only wished he would stay close to the vine and keep our life and marriage covered. But my fear right now was that he had taken his eye off Christ and the potential downfall that it could bring.

'Til death do us part right? I had a job, a home that I loved, friends, and now I once again had to pick up and leave for my husband regardless of how I felt about it. I was disgusted but felt I had no choice. He left in January of that year and came back to Dayton to move our belongings in May of that year. He made me feel like I was the worst person in the world when he left for that five-month span. The way he addressed me and the way he acted when he was around me alone would totally contradict how he would tell others that he loved me. To others, especially his sisters, I was negative and trying to control him. As usual, I noticed but didn't say anything. This unhealthy cycle of silence continued as I sought to keep peace.

We had been married almost 30 years by now and overall, Franklin was a very sweet and gentle for the most part. We had a good marriage overall. For most of our family life, we had meals together, we prayed together every night, we attended church regularly, we had a couple friends that we could have fun with, we had jobs that provided for all our needs. It was heartbreaking to see such a change in the man I love.

Like most women of my generation, I was completely dependent on him for everything, and I guess I trusted him too much. That was just how I was raised and what was modeled for me by the prior two generations. He was in control of my life, and I desperately needed to figure out how to protect myself and I wanted to protect him too as I loved him unconditionally. He did not choose this illness and my wedding vows were in sickness and in health. But now, I feel like it is important for me to start saving money from my job so that he won't spend all of that. I can't seem to find a predictable pattern and I could anticipate the problems to come.

We were in a lot of debt when he left Ohio and I didn't know how bad it was until he picked me up. I had to pay the moving bill out of my personal account because his was empty. We stayed with our son, Lyle, on Merritt Island, Florida for seven months because we had to wait for the house to sell in Ohio in order to qualify to buy another home since he had run up all of his credit card bills that quickly. When we sold the house, we took extra money out against the house to pay off some of the bills. Once I got a job with the Paralyzed Veterans of America (PVA), we started a joint account. One visa was so high, and the balance hardly moved after making payments for months. I felt like I was always doing damage control and that I cared more about his credit than he did. I still ended up using what little savings I did have to pay off his debt just for him to turn around and dig another hole.

21

Money, Money, Money, Money…

*"Abide in me, and I in you.
As the branch cannot bear fruit by itself,
unless it abides in the vine, neither can you,
unless you abide in me."*

— JOHN 15:4 —

The man I fell in love with, married, and bore his children is gone. I don't see him in his eyes, his speech is different, and his behavior is starting to scare me. Despite him continuing to function at work, the next three years would be the scariest, most unpredictable, and hardest three years of my life. What is even more bizarre is that he will not even remember doing these things.

Looking back, I think the root of our problems was always money. When Franklin was experiencing mania, it was like money became his addiction. He would do just about anything to get what he wanted once he had his mind made up even if he did not have the money. Whether it was the boat, a car, electronics, or just doing something for some random stranger, he was going to figure out how to do what he wanted to do regardless of how I felt about it. If he pressured me to agree with him and I refused, rest assured he would beg, borrow, or steal to get it. When I say steal, I don't mean like a criminal but to me if you overextend your credit knowing you can't afford the payments and you end up filing bankruptcy, then you are stealing from that business that trusted you to pay that bill when they provided you a product, even if it is legal to do so. We had not filed bankruptcy and I never intend to but that is where Franklin was headed if he did not stop using credit.

People living with bipolar disorder have challenges with impulsivity. That may play out in a variety of ways like poor decision making in business, relationships, spending, and even in charity or giving to others. These behaviors can show up in both mania and bouts of depression. Over-spending tends to get people in deep holes which then leads to regret, guilt, and depression.

The more I tried to pay-off our debts and curb his spending, the angrier he got with me and that led to his resentment towards me. He seemed to believe I was trying to take away his freedom and control what he called HIS money because he certainly earned the majority of the income in our household. I couldn't seem to get him to understand that I was trying my best to help him and protect our future by avoiding bankruptcy or worse. Now that Franklin's been away from the Word and church for about a year or more and he was refusing to take any meds, his money crazed behavior was spiraling out of control.

I often got confused wondering if his behavior was really the bi-polar or if he was just being a rebellious man. If he was really that sick from bi-polar how was he doing so well at work and socially? Funny how you don't see the power and control issues of the man you love until you look back on things. Once I got tired of the reckless financial behavior, I put my foot down about his spending and insisted that I manage our bills. Little did I know this would start a series of incidents that were passive aggressive at first but them became down right life threatening. This whole downwards spiral started because I feared homelessness, yet he seemed to fear subordination to his wife.

The first major financial incident came when a female employee at the Veterans outpatient clinic where we both worked named Sally Washington. Franklin was an employee assistance counselor at the clinic, and she sought help to get out of an abusive relationship. She had two young children and needed a new place to live but did not have any money to buy furniture. "Do gooder" Franklin decided he was going to purchase a house full of furniture for her with the promise that she would make the payments. It was placed on our credit card, so the company called me at work to notify me when they were delivering it.

I was at work and the phone rang. I answered the telephone and a male voice said,

"Can I speak to Mrs. Hendricks?"

"This is Mrs. Hendricks," I said hesitantly wondering who this person was.

He continued, "I need some directions to your house."

I asked, "For what?" not knowing who he was and why on earth he needed to know where I lived.

He said, "We are trying to deliver your furniture that you or your husband ordered."

I said confused, not knowing he ordered furniture, "I did not order any furniture."

He pressed on, "Are you Sally Hendricks?"

"No, my name is Virginia Hendricks."

"Is your husband's name Franklin?" he asked.

"Yes, it is," I replied with a sick feeling in my stomach and dread that tasted up like vomit.

"Well, we have a washer, dryer, and living room furniture on our truck along with some other items to deliver," he continued with not sensing my uneasiness or dread.

I asked hoping that he had the wrong Hendricks or anything but what I knew was beginning to fear, "What address do you have?"

When he read the address, I told him "That is not my address."

With a slight sense of relief and the sickness that she was feeling was subsiding because I thought that meant they called the wrong person.

"Well, this is the address we were told to deliver to, but it is in Franklin and Sally Hendricks's name," he said.

I said hoping this was an error, but she knew it wasn't and was beginning to feel the sickness in the pit of her stomach returning, dreading the outcome of her investigation, "I think you better take it back to the store until I get to the bottom of this." I asked for the salesman's name so I could call Sears and check on this. He gave me his name as I felt anger growing.

I hung up the phone, picked it back up and called Sears to ask for the salesman. I told him about what had been discussed with the men that were trying to deliver furniture that I did not order. He asked me to hold on while he looked up the information on the sale. He came back and said,

"This order was part of the order and the rest had been delivered a week earlier."

Totally confused and beginning to feel angry I asked, "What was delivered earlier?"

He looked at the sales slip and read off the items that were delivered,

"Bedroom furniture, living room furniture, and some miscella-neous stuff."

"Well, someone is in trouble, and I plan to get to the bottom of this. Do you remember what the lady looked like?" I asked with curiosity because I only know one Sally.

He tried to describe her and said she had a child with her as well.

"That truly is not me and all of my children are grown," I told him the purchase was a fraud and he needed to report it.

"Ma'am, I really do not want to be involved in this because I was just doing my job," he insisted.

He asked me to talk to his boss and put him on the phone. I explained the problem and told him that I wanted to find out who signed the bill when the purchase was made. He gave me a number to call and said they could pull it up on their computer and give me the information I wanted. By this time, I was very nervous and upset and needed to get out of this building. I had to go home and make these calls because people were walking in my office, and I did not want anyone listening to the conversation. I was so angry and embarrassed and moving into crisis mode.

My husband was out of town so I could not get ahold of him. I rushed home and started making phone calls. The second lady I talked to was very helpful and gave me a lot of information. We had a long talk about the information that I had gotten from the store earlier that day.

She said, "The name of the lady with your husband was Sally Washington. Do you know her?"

"No, I don't but I have an idea who it might be, and she may work in the same place as me and my husband," I said.

"Did she give a phone number," I asked.

"Yes, if you promise not to give my name, I will give it to you," she pleaded knowing she could lose her job for giving out this information but hearing the desperation in my voice, wanted to help me.

"I promise I will not mention you when I call her," I assured her.

"Please calm down before you make the call," fearing that I would be irrational and say or do something that I might later regret.

"I wil.l" I told her.

When I made the call, I thought I recognized the voice.

I asked, "Are you Sally that works in reception at the clinic?"

She answered that she was. I told her who I was, and asked, "Have you been shopping for furniture with my husband?"

Yes, he didn't tell you?"

"No, he did not. Do you want to tell me what's going on here?"

"He said he was going to tell you."

"Tell me what?"I asked as I felt myself getting physically and emotionally upset and I just had to hang up before finishing this conversation for fear that I was going to lose my temper.

I started making phone calls to Sears credit department. I found out that most of the items had been purchased in Daytona Beach, and that it was not all purchased at the same time. They had been in that store a few times, and it was always on weekends. I could not believe I was having to go through this.

When Franklin returned home, I approached him with this, and he admitted what he had done.

"We did nothing wrong," he said. "The lady needed help, she can't get credit, so I helped her buy what she needed."

"You got a house full of furniture!", I screamed. "Are you planning on moving in with her? I asked.

"No!", he said. "Why would you say that?" he asked.

"You're buying all new furniture for her and nothing for me, you must be going to stay with her." I insisted not sure if I really wanted to know the truth but not being able to stop myself from asking.

"She is going to pay for it."

"What if she doesn't pay for it?"

"Then I will have to pay for it," he replied like it was no big deal.

"If you make one payment on that furniture you better make arrangements to live someplace because I don't want you here," I screamed.

The men that were trying to deliver the furniture took it back to the store after they talked to me earlier that day. The following weekend Franklin took Sally to another store. This time it was Levitz furniture store. It would be a few weeks before I found out about that. I called one of their stores and asked if the purchase had been made in Franklin's name in the past few weeks.

He asked me to let him pull it up on the computer and then he said "Yes, the purchase was made at another store, and I can give you that number if you want."

I was devastated. "Yes, I would like that very much, thank you."

He gave me the number and I made a call to find out that a new account had been made in Franklin and Sally's name together. This almost blew my mind. I don't know why I was surprised. He always figures out how to get what he wants without considering my feelings.

I asked calmly knowing there was nothing I could do at this point, "Well can you tell me what was purchased?"

Her answer was, "Why sure, a dryer, furniture for the kid's room, and they special ordered a bedroom suite which will be ready in a few days."

I told her that I was Mrs. Hendricks and that my name was not Sally. At that point, she didn't want to give me any more information. I don't blame her. I told her to advise her store not to deliver the furniture. She said that she would talk to her manager. I asked her to put a statement in the computer that if the bill is not being paid never call my house because I will not pay on that bill and I have control of the checkbook.

Franklin was back and forth at home sometimes and on the boat at other times but right now he was home. As if that new Sears encounter was not enough, two weeks later I went to the bank to check on things and learned that $900 was missing from our account. Just as I found out, the phone rang, it was my daughter, Belinda. We talked about 30 minutes about how things were going for her in Atlanta then I said I have to hang up now, but I would be in touch. I didn't want to tell her about this mess. I hung up the phone and went to get the account numbers so I could check to see if the bills were being paid. I was anxious and fearing that we were going to end up homeless.

When I walked into the bedroom, I saw his wallet laying on the nightstand, it was like a voice said, "open it". I stood there for a moment; I had never done this before. I was thinking no, but then I turned around, picked the wallet up, opened it and the first thing I saw was a new temporary sears credit card and several $100.00 bills. I wondered what in the world was he up to now? When I confronted him, he claimed that his sister, Frances, had borrowed it. Knowing that was not typical for my sister-in-law who usually came through me to borrow money, I decided to call her. As expected, Frances reported that this story was untrue. So now he is lying to try and cover up what he is really doing. This is so exhausting to have to check and double check everything the man I love and depend on says to me. When I confronted Franklin about this lie, he stated he went to Orange Blossom Trail and started handing out cash to prostitutes.

Next think I know, Franklin had been to the bank and took out all of the money we had in our joint account. I went to the bank to check on our accounts, savings, vacation and checking and found out that he took everything except just enough to keep the account open. I couldn't believe I was going through this. I tried to talk to him about taking the money from the account and find out why he did it. I asked what he did with the money and he simply said he had spent it.

He said he gave to people who needed it, but most of it "was spent in bars," he said. "You know how it is when you get around a lot of guys," he added.

"No, I don't but I want you to tell me."

"We take turns buying rounds."

He moved out of the house that day and I don't know where he was staying but I was told he was at our boat. I was so angry that I didn't even care. I was planning on going to my son's wedding which was in a few days. I continued my plans and asked if he was going with me.

He said, "No, I don't want to go."

I wasn't surprised but disappointed for my son who expected his family to be at his wedding. He called me after I got to work that day and asked when I was leaving. I said this afternoon after work, and he said that he would take me to the bus station. I told him I didn't know what I was going to do when I got back home. I was so disappointed that he was not going to come with me and that I had to be dropped off at a bus station in the first place. I don't even own a car and my entire life is turned upside down right now.

I left and went to a friend's house and spent the night because I was too angry to sleep in the same house with him since he was still coming in and out getting things. I went to the wedding and had a lovely time despite being very upset. All five of our children were there and they looked so beautiful and happy for Lester. I had to try and put on a happy face although it was very hard. So many emotions stirring within. After the wedding was over, they started asking about how their dad was doing and why he didn't come to the wedding. I had already told our youngest daughter, Belinda, about what happened so I thought I may as well tell all of them that dad was not doing so good. I told them that he moved out and he came back home the night before I was leaving for Atlanta. They continued to ask questions I couldn't answer, and I don't think they fully understood how serious this was because over the years I never really said much about this.

The following week I got a call from Sears again. They asked to speak to Mrs. Hendricks and the operator put the call through to me.

They were actually looking for Sally instead of me. The man started talking about some things that were bought on Saturday by Franklin. I informed him that Franklin was on vacation Friday and asked if he was sure he was in the store on Saturday He confirmed that Franklin was. I also asked but knew the answer, if someone else was with him and he told me that he was with a lady and a child.

When I asked what they bought he said a microwave and a TV. I asked to talk to his manager, and it turned out to be one of the men I had talked to before. I introduced myself and reminded him that I had talked to him before. He remembered and he pulled the file. Then he came back to the phone and said the credit card was used Saturday and signed by Sally Hendricks. I confirmed the credit card number by reading it to him and he told me that this was the same number. Since she fraudulently signed a non-existent name on my account, the manager asked me to talk to one of the security people. I explained that this person was using my husband's credit card and that my husband was out of town on vacation. He wanted to know if I knew who she was, so I explained that she worked in the same building that I did. He listened and then suggested that I talk to her and ask her to return those items by tomorrow and if she did, they wouldn't press charges.

I decided to call here right then and asked that he stay on the line and listen. I called her extension from my office phone and told her that I talked to the Sears security department and told them that somebody was using Franklin's credit card.

Do you have his card?"

"Yes, I do."

"Did you use it on Saturday?"

"Yes, I did."

"Okay, I know what you bought, they already told me. Now, if you take those items back, they may not press charges against you but, you must have them back by noon Tuesday.

"Next thing, do you want to give me my husband's credit card or would you rather I call the police?"

She said, "I will give it to you."

"I want it today," I told her.

"Okay I'll bring it over to your office."

Then she hung up the phone. The man was still on the phone, and he said, "If she brings it back, I'll let you know." Later that week, on Wednesday, he called to tell me that she did return the microwave and TV. I was still angry but at least I felt like someone understood and was willing to help. I thanked him for his help.

This was the beginning of the end for our marriage. The traditional old school southern man was a sexist and believed the husband was the head of the household in all aspects including finances. He was used to doing what he wanted all his life. He didn't care what his parents or anyone else thought. He married a young southern woman who never questioned him and always believed in him and now she is standing up to him and taking over his authority in the home and I knew he was not about to accept that. It is not about who is the head of the home anymore. This is a survival tactic to address an illness that is altering his ability to lead our home.

Franklin packed his car one Friday evening told me he was going to Alabama. I asked if he was going to drive all night and he said until he gets tired. Once again, I was left at home for a weekend without a car because we were still sharing one vehicle. Two days after he left, I called VISA to check on the balance. I had paid the card off about two months before he left and now, I was told the current balance was $1700.00. I felt so defeated and helpless! I tried to explain to the creditor what was going on with Franklin, his inability to stop his spending due to his mental health, but she didn't seem to believe me and told me his name was on the card and he had the right to use it as he wished. I made eleven calls that morning. On the eleventh call I said my visa card was stolen. Then I got some results, she took my card and said they would issue another card. I asked her to wait to hear from me before she sent the card. Less than an hour later, I received a call from Franklin fussing me out because the bank had taken his card in Montgomery, Alabama. I called my local bank and had them hold enough money to cover the checks that I had already sent out to pay bills. He came home the next morning, went to the bank, tried to draw everything out but was told there was hold on some of it to cover outstanding checks. He got angry, called me, and fussed me out again. I know he isn't well, but I really am trying to protect him, and he can't see it. He had talked to our baby girl and told her that he was going to draw all the money out of the bank so the checks would bounce. She tried to talk to him about how hurtful that was, but he wouldn't listen, so she called to give me a heads up.

It is so hard and confusing, and even scary to watch the man I love become someone I don't recognize. I'm sure I will never know the whole truth behind some of this and perhaps that's best at this point because these two years of my life would be the most bizarre and even scary times for our family. It would be a time of uncharacteristic behavior from him emotionally, financially, ethically, morally, and totally different from the kind-hearted, loving preacher's kid I fell in love with.

"Where are you going Franklin?"

"Out," he murmured.

"Out where?"

"I don't know", just out" he barked.

"How long will you be gone? You know we only have one car."

"I don't know Virginia!" he yelled. "Why do you care anyway? I will be back before work on Monday," he said as he slammed the garage door.

I sat silently as the car cranked and the outside garage door closed as he drove away. The tears started to well up in my eyes, then anger started to cause me to feel warm and my heart started racing.

"How did I get to this point?", I asked myself. I have loved Franklin since I was 19 years old. Almost 36 years later and I am angry at myself because I have allowed myself to be totally dependent upon him and now, I feel helpless. I have never purchased a car, a home, and I don't even have a credit card in just my name. I have totally trusted him with my livelihood and for the first time I don't feel secure. So here I am for yet another weekend, stranded in my own home, and too ashamed to call anyone to tell them what I have been dealing with for the past several months. I don't know where he went, who he's with, or what he is doing. I have never had to think about that before because we have typically always been together when we were not at work. Now, he is treating me like a mistress and not a soul mate. "What is going on?" I asked myself. I don't know what I should do other than pray.

Franklin showed up late Sunday evening. He came in the house, went to our room, and went to bed without either of us saying a word. The next day started off with what I considered to be "normal", whatever that means anymore. Nothing is truly "normal" around here.

We got up early, got dressed left for work as usual without even speaking to each other. We rode together in complete silence since we worked in the same building and we only have one car. I wanted my own car but doubted I could get one on my own since I had never purchased a major item on my own throughout my life, so I feel a bit lost, helpless, and frustrated and literally at his mercy and he knew it. I prayed this would never happen to my daughters.

I was 55 years old, in a dead marriage, to a man I no longer trust. It was almost a relief to get to work for some socialization and relaxation, but the days went too fast. I fretted going home every evening and it would cause anxiety because I never knew what mood he would be in or what behavior to expect.

We arrived home about the same time as we usually did just before 5:00 p.m. Franklin went to the bedroom, changed his clothes, and went to bed before dinner. This is not unusual for him, and in fact he had been doing this a lot over the last few weeks stating he just "felt bad" and he was always tired. This is what depression looks like. Although he would go to bed early, he would wake up around the time I went to bed between 10 and 11pm and get up to watch the television or listening to music on the stereo which would make it hard for me to sleep. It also made me wonder if he was just avoiding me by going to bed. I knew if I said anything, he would just get very upset. No matter what or how I said things to him he always got angry. It's like walking through life on eggshells and unfortunately keeping a lot inside. Eventually those emotions just build and eventually you just can't take it anymore.

22

The Final Admission

*"But when he heard it, he said,
"Those who are well have no need of a physician,
but those who are sick."*

— MATTHEW 9:12 —

It finally got to the point where we all believed he needed to go back to the hospital for help. The laws regarding psychiatric admissions protect the patient. Unless Franklin agreed to an admission, we would have to convince an officer or the court that he was a threat to self or someone else and even with that he would only stay in the hospital for two to three days. Lyle and I tried making multiple phone calls to see if there was anything else we could do on his behalf. The bottom line was consistent that unless we could prove without a doubt that he was suicidal or homicidal he would have to agree to go into the hospital voluntarily. I understand the reasons behind consumer protection, and

I can imagine that rights may be violated without those protections but as a family member afraid for my safety and his I once again feel helpless and concerned. I called the rest of the children to let them know what was going on. My baby girl said she was coming home and would try to get him to voluntarily go into the hospital for an assessment. I told her he was due back on Sunday from Alabama. She came down on Sunday and got here about two hours before he did. She talked to him that evening for a long time. She tried to explain in detail why we were all worried about him and felt he needed to reconsider returning to treatment. Then we all went to bed. The next morning, I got up and started to get ready for work. Belinda said she was going to call the doctor to see if he would see him on that day. I left work at 8:30 AM as usual. Belinda called me at work to tell me they were going to Rockledge to see dad's doctor. Franklin was not comfortable using the VA because he worked there and was convinced that other employees would read his record, so he insisted on going to a private inpatient facility outside of Orlando. Later she called me to let me know that he would be staying in the hospital for a few days. The doctor admitted him only because he voluntarily agreed.

Belinda assisted him with admission and getting settled before returning to my house. She had to leave early the next day for Atlanta so that she could return to work and get back to school. She said she would fill me in on everything when she got home. I gave her directions how to get back home from the East coast since she was not familiar with this area.

Franklin stayed in the hospital for a few days but because Belinda left and went back to Atlanta, he seemed to have resentment towards her for several years, as if she abandoned him. Their relationship would never be the same which was sad because they share the same career, have similar compassionate hearts for the underdog, and she definitely has his smile.

He was also angry at me and Lyle because he felt like we were trying to get guardianship and take away his rights and independence. I am not sure where he got that idea but there was no convincing him otherwise.

This admission would be Franklin's last effort for treatment for his bipolar disorder, at least during our marriage, and our lives would forever change. Treatment had sustained him off and on over the years. The absence of treatment and the decline of his faith walk meant that he would likely not be in control of many decisions and I don't know how we can survive a constant roller coaster of uncertainty, fear, and his reckless behavior with money. For the first time in our marriage, I entertained the reality that I may not be able to keep our vows.

Belinda arrived back in Orlando around 9:00 PM looking sad.

"What's wrong," I asked?

She said, "I don't think he needed to be there and not sure he is that bad."

"Well why did you leave him there?"

"Because you and the doctor think he needs to be there."

"Hey, I didn't tell you to have him admitted," I said defensively.

"I thought it may help for him to get some help because of what he did. I don't think it's normal behavior."

Belinda said, "he didn't want me to leave so I stayed as long as I could and tried to comfort him as much as possible, but I could tell how hurt he was when I left."

She was telling me how bad some of those people where and that dad did not seem bad enough to be in there with them. I felt really bad that she had to go through that and that she seemed to feel so guilty, but I had been the bad guy all this time because I didn't agree with the things he was doing. It was a relief for me to have him out of the house because I was very angry about his spending, he had been leaving me at home on weekends without a car and buying a house full of furniture for a lady. I had worked very hard trying to get some of the bills paid off so we could start enjoying ourselves. I had tried that before and now I was thinking what's the use? Why do I keep doing this to myself when I know it's not going to work? It was a pattern that I knew, but I didn't want to accept it. I was sorry Belinda felt badly, but I also think he was manipulating her.

I kept in touch with the hospital through the social worker and his doctor. While at work one day, I had a call from the hospital telling me to get rid of Franklin's guns. He had three of them in our bedroom, one pistol and two old shotguns from his grandfather.

"Why do I need to remove the guns?" I asked.

They told me to just get them all out of my house before Franklin was discharged. No need to ask why. There is one gun in the master bedroom closet with a special bullet that Franklin used to say would blow a person's head off. There's also a sword under our bed and they told me to move it as well. By now, I am really getting nervous. They also mentioned a handgun and rifle in the closet. Now I had the shakes. If they knew all of that they obviously heard it from Franklin. I asked if there was anything else I needed to know?

"This is confidential information. I am sticking my neck out by telling you this, but I thought you should know."

"Thank you very much and I do appreciate the information," I replied.

Belinda told me that they only do that if they have a legal "duty to warn" and this is usually associated with suicidal or homicidal threats. The counselor had an obligation to warn me that I was potentially in danger but they could not violate privacy so they could not give me full details. Franklin had expressed homicidal ideations years earlier in Albuquerque directed at co-workers. Now, I am left wondering if he was trying to harm himself or me. Either way, I called Lyle to come and get the guns out of the house.

Lyle picked his dad up from the hospital and brought him home. Franklin was very quiet and distant, perhaps hurt, that we all felt he needed to be in that place.

"Franklin how are you feeling?"

"I am here and in the land of the living", he said.

"You seem upset", I said.

"I am."

"What are you upset about?"

"I can't believe you and Lyle want to take guardianship over me", He murmured.

"I am not crazy. I am competent, and I am perfectly capable of managing my own affairs."

"No one called you crazy Franklin," I assured him. "Guardianship was discussed only to try and help protect you from continuing to make decisions that could potentially harm us financially. "If you keep doing the things you are doing, we will lose everything. Is that what you want?"

"I would rather lose everything, then have you control my life."

"If that is how you feel about it then maybe you should just go back to the boat."

I decided to not say anything else as I knew from the past, this conversation would just escalate. He ate dinner and went back to the east coast with Lyle and I could tell he was angry and that I would be in for more drama.

23

Rejections Fury

*"A joyful heart is good medicine,
but a crushed spirit dries up the bones."*

— PROVERBS 17:22 —

Two months after Franklin left home, he came into my office handed me a booklet from the courts downtown with instructions on how to get a quick divorce. This may be the only way not to lose the house. If we separate our debts, perhaps they won't force me to move and only hold me accountable for my debts. Two days later, Franklin told me he had spent over $20,000.00 on credit cards in the past 2 months.

"Who are you spending so much money on?" I asked.

He said, "I am spending it in bars and on whoever needs it."

One week later, he took a vacation and went to North Carolina and Alabama with some of his drinking friends. I never did meet any of these friends but according to him they were very good friends. He could not see that they were using him as long as he was flashing those credit cards. I tried to talk to him about his spending, but every time he would get very hostile when I mentioned anything about money.

Rejection sensitivity for individuals with bipolar can result in emotional distress. An example of rejection sensitivity would be if a person is perceived as not liking them, it is seen as rejection but instead of moving on they may lash out, push people away in a painful way or potentially a more dramatic angry reaction. For Franklin, me, or anyone else telling him no or trying to stop him from doing what he wants to do seems to cause a stress reaction within him that results in symptoms like chronic pain, depression and harassment and verbal abuse of me. Even though Franklin voluntarily left our home on more than one occasion, his story was that I rejected him and put him out and somehow that became his truth and his truth led to anger and rage and destructive behavior. Every week I never knew when I would be subjected to his harassment or verbally abusive behavior and because we worked in the same building, there was no escaping.

The next week Franklin came into my office and did not speak. That hurt me very much, I didn't think I deserved that from him. I called him later in the day just to say hi and that led into an argument. I got angry because he was trying to make me feel guilty for him leaving me.

The next day I had been thinking about Franklin's sickness, wondering again how a person works his job if he is sick as I thought he was. Maybe he just wanted out of our marriage I would tell myself, but why didn't he just say that? I could handle that so much better than the treatment he was giving me. It was so hard for me to understand the things he was doing because he was always so good to me.

Franklin's boss came to my office the next morning asking, "Have you seen Franklin?"

"No, I have not," I replied.

"Well, he didn't come to work, and he is not answering his pager, so I wanted to see if he was ok."

"I have not seen or heard from him today," I told him.

When he left to go back to his office, I got on the phone and called our son Lyle and asked if he had seen his dad's car when he passed the yacht club. I told him he didn't show up for work and he said he would drive down to the boat to check on him on his way to work. Lyle found him in the boat and told him that his boss was looking for him. He told Lyle that he was supposed to be off that day. Later, Franklin called his boss and said he was off, and it was approved.

That afternoon I went to talk to his boss again. "Franklin says he talked to you?"

"Yes, we talked, and I approved his leave for today, thanks Virginia."

"I am worried about him. Do you think there is anything that you can do to help Franklin?"

"Not unless he messes up on the job," he responded. "And so far, he has not done that."

Then I began to think he was just doing what he wanted to do. If he was that sick, there would be no way for him to do so well on the job. I still couldn't fully understand how bipolar was episodic and not constant so there were times when things seem "normal" but just not lately.

Thinking back over the last few months, things had not been so good between us, but I did not realize it at the time. He was at the place where he didn't want to do anything that I wanted to do. He was always trying to make me feel that I was wrong in almost everything that I did. He never talked to me as a friend. If he talked at all it was always to do this or do that for him. I was becoming his slave even though he thought I was trying to make him mine.

The next day was a peaceful day at work because Franklin was on sick leave. But when I got home, I had a big surprise. There were tracks all over the floor, none of my phones were working, the appliances were out, and both TV would not turn on. I was by myself and almost panicked. I ran next door to use the phone and called the police. Turned out the house was struck by lightning. I told Franklin about our house being struck by lightning. It did not seem to bother him at all. I had already called the insurance company and they had given me a time to meet the insurance adjuster at my house. I asked if he would go over and meet me there because I didn't know what I was looking for. After the inspection was over, I tried to talk to him, but he never wanted to talk about his problems because he would say he "had too many".

I asked him to draw up a statement relieving me from all debts that he had run up while he was running the streets. He said he was about $19-20k in debt since he left home. Since my telephones were out, I went over to the shopping center to use a pay phone to let the kids know what was going on and when I returned, he had taken a bath and dyed his hair black. Then he left without saying anything. The next day we talked on the telephone about the house problems. I told him that I was going to Sears after work to buy a telephone. By the time I got to Sears, he was there and had picked out two telephones for me to buy. After I paid for them, he put them in my car and left.

Saturday, I spent the night with a friend and when I returned home on Sunday afternoon Franklin was at our house washing his clothes and had already cut the grass. When I walked in, he said he was getting ready to leave and he would get out of my way. I asked why he would say that. He said it was because of the way I looked at him when I walked in. He looks so bad, and I asked if I could cut his hair. He said ok, if I wanted to. He got the clippers for me, I cut his hair then he was in a hurry to leave.

A new work week and five minutes after I got to work, he called and asked, "How much is in the bank?"

"Let me remind you of how many checks have not cleared since you checked last week," I said. He just hung up.

Later that day he stopped by my office.

"I have pizza, would you like some?", he asked.

"Sure, thank you", I replied.

As we had lunch together, he asked, "How are the telephones?".

"The lines were fixed, and the phones were working fine now," I answered. "The jacks had burned out from the lightning."

A little later in the day, he called and asked, "Do you think Lyle would loan me some money?"

"I have no idea; you should call Lyle."

Franklin said, "I need the money to help pay on a plaque for one of my coworkers that's leaving for another job. "

I offered to loan him the money for that. He came right down, and I gave him $20. He was so happy that he left my office just as fast has he had come there.

I took Friday off from work that week to go fishing with some friends. When I returned home, he had been in my house and left a note saying that he had taken a bath and was leaving for Gainesville with a male friend for the weekend. On Saturday I went to a family reunion in Tampa. When I returned home on Sunday afternoon he was in my house in the bed. Our son Lyle and his family were there also. He got out of bed at 9 pm and went into the kitchen, cooked some sausage, made a sandwich and went back to bed in the guestroom.

The following morning, he got up early and left without saying anything. After I got to work, he came into my office and asked for a dollar, I reached into my purse and handed him $2. Later he stopped by and asked about my fishing trip. We sat there and talked for about two minutes about my fishing trip.

Lyle and I had a long talk about his dad taking two women to Alabama when he went on vacation. He had also taken these two women to Disney World. He had taken lots of trips with men. He had talked to me about some of his male friends, some were out of state. He had made visits to Virginia, Washington DC, Baltimore, Louisiana, and North Carolina. He was having so much fun with male friends that I began to think he was a homosexual. After all, his sex drive was almost at the bottom with me for years and he never had any desire for sex. I used to wonder, what was wrong with me? I am attractive, I dress well, but he just didn't want me as a sex partner anymore. I tried to tell myself that it was his sickness.

Now I am not so sure since he has been seen with other women and lots of men. There was a group of men that used to meet on the boat for wild parties, drinking all kinds of alcohol and watching xx rated movies. Some of these movies contained scenes where men were having sex with men and women with women. I was having a hard time believing this. I asked my son to go by and check to see if this was true but when he did the locks had been changed and he couldn't get in. Another day he went back there and one of Franklin's friends was there filling the cooler with ice and beer. Lyle went on the boat and looked around, saw a box of video tapes picked up a couple and they were X rated. On another day he went there, and two men were lying down watching some of those movies in the middle of the day.

I tried to make conversation with Franklin when I saw him, but he made it so hard sometimes because he just refused to be honest with me. Next time I saw Franklin,

I asked, "How did you enjoy your visit at Disney with your friend?"

He said, "I didn't go to Disney."

"Oh who did you buy the tickets for?" I asked.

"No one!" he yelled.

I said, "A friend saw you buying tickets with your friend.I got my phone bill, and you made a call from Disney and charged it to my bill."

"I have already called that number to find out where it was coming from and it was inside of Disney grounds." I added.

Then he turned and said, "I never said I didn't go to Disney."

Not much happened the next day. A few days later he called to see if I had any mail for him. I didn't have any, but I did offer some cupcakes and he came right down and seemed happy.

I called him later that week and started talking and what a mistake that was. I was accused of being negative in everything I said, I always cut him down, and he was not coming home to be treated that way. He said he was happy on the houseboat. I asked him to please get some help so he could get himself together. He said he was not sick. I told him I was waiting for him to say that because I didn't see how he could function as well as he does on the job if he was as sick as he seemed to be. I also asked if he could come over to the house and be there with me when the man came to do an estimate for fixing the house. He said he would if he got out of court on time.

When I got home, he was there waiting. I tried to talk to him but not much good came out of that. He only wanted to talk about things that upset me. He began to tell me how much money he was spending. I don't know how far in debt he was, but he said he had been spending over $100 per day. When asked what he was doing to spend that much he didn't have a good answer and said he was just trying to survive. He admitted to having fun with friends and drinking in bars.

The gentleman from home improvement came and checked the house over from the lightning strike, he gave us an estimate and left. We began to talk again, and he assured me that he was not sick. He got up and got dressed and said he was leaving. Then he asked me if I had eaten? I had not so he left and came back with two dinners, one for each of us. We sat there and ate together, mostly in silence with very little small talk. After he finished, he got comfortable on the sofa and spent the night in the guestroom. The following morning, he got up and went to work. He left before I did because he had to report to work earlier. I didn't see much of him that day. He did come to my office and asked if I called the insurance company and I assured him that I had taken care of that.

Friday, he called me at home before I was ready for work and wanted to know how much money he had in the bank. I didn't know because it was hard for me to keep up with it when he withdrew so much out and did not tell me. He got angry and hung up. I called back and tried to explain to him that I was not using his money for anything except to pay some of his bills.

"I'll never talk to you about money again", I told him before hanging up.

A little later he walked into my office and put a note on my desk stating he deducted $50 from our account. All I could do was shake my head.

Saturday was a peaceful day. I had no contact with him. Sunday evening called and asked if he could come over and wash his clothes. He was on I-4 coming from the Cape. That was an odd answer since I-4 is in a different direction. He came over, washed his clothes, and went to bed in the guestroom.

Monday morning, he got up and went to work. That afternoon he went back to my house to finish cutting the grass. After he finished, he came inside and went to bed. He got up Tuesday morning and went to work.

Later that day, I was involved in a car accident after work and had to be taken to the hospital. Someone hit me in the back while I was stopped at a red light. I had no idea how to get in contact with him. I never felt so alone in my life. I even tried to call a couple of friends and couldn't get in contact with anyone. This was my first accident ever.

The next morning, he called me before I was out of bed telling me to get a pen and paper to write something down because he was in trouble. I said to him that I was in trouble myself as I was in an accident the night before. I don't even know if he heard me because he didn't respond and continued to focus on what he needed.

After a moment of silence, I asked, "What do you want me to write down?"

Of course, it was about money. He is so far in debt he could not pay his bills. He asked if I would pay his credit union bill. I agreed to pay it for that month. He called me that night to see how I was feeling. I told him I felt pretty good, and he said he would call back but never did. At least I knew he heard me earlier, but I felt like he was only being nice because I agreed to pay that bill for him.

Another month went by and the same type of up and down in our relationship continued and I continued to worry about him. He was as he says "surviving" but it just did not seem healthy, and he just kept heading for trouble financially and emotionally. One day, Franklin asked if he could come over to cut the grass. After he finished, he went in and took a bath, laid down on the sofa and watched television. I tried to talk to him about getting professional help, trying to make him understand that he could not fight this battle without help. He started telling me that he was doing what he wanted to do.

I said, "Even though you hurt me deeply you don't care, you don't feel anything about me."

He didn't believe that he did anything to hurt me and restated that he was just doing what he wanted to do. I told him that if after all he had done, and he didn't care than he should be leaving this home. Of course, he got angry, started fussing, and picking up his clothes stating he would never put his feet in our house again. He got everything together and left. About an hour and a half later the doorbell rang. It was Franklin. He needed to use the bathroom and get a drink of water. I let him in. He did both and left again. A few minutes later, two of my sisters drove up in the driveway. I looked out the window to see who was out there and he was helping them get their bags out of the car. He brought them in the house using his key as if nothing was going on. He sat on the couch talking to everyone as though he still lived here.

I was sitting at the table, he got up off the sofa, came over and kissed me on the jaw like he used to act, as though he had been there all the time. When he got tired, he went to bed in my bedroom and never said a word. He got up the next morning and went to work without saying a word to anyone. I didn't know how to handle all this acting normal in front of guests. I didn't want to upset him in front of my family. I knew it would not last long, so I just let it go. That afternoon he didn't come back over and he didn't call.

24

More Money

*"He who loves money will not be satisfied with money,
nor he who loves wealth with his income; this also is vanity."*

— ECCLESIASTES 5:10 —

As I mentioned before, money is a major source of stress in our relationship and seems to be the key issue of concern for Franklin. It's like he thinks money makes everything OK. It also seems to be a source of his anger. Since I have had my own account with my own money for years and even though it isn't much, he doesn't seem to want me to have any money. He constantly comes to me for money as if it is some type of power play. I don't think he will be happy until we are both broke and destitute. And yet, I don't set boundaries and I continue to help him and give him what he wants even when it doesn't make any sense. In some ways I feel sorry for him and in other ways I feel indebted to him, and I am still his wife.

Franklin called me after I got to work saying "Babe will you loan me $150.00 until Wednesday?"

I started to write the check but realized in the register that there was not enough money to cover it.

I told him "I am sorry Franklin, but I didn't have that much money."

He was not happy at all and I felt like he did not believe me. I did not hear from him on Saturday or Sunday but Monday morning he called me at work and said he was in Alabama. When I got off work, I called his aunt in Montgomery and asked if she had seen him, but she had not seen or heard from him. I wondered where he really was and who he was with because she is the only person in Alabama on his side of the family that he visits when he goes to Alabama.

The next day he called again from Alabama and said he was visiting some friend that he had met when he was in Montgomery before. He then told me he wanted to come home. I said to him that he was going about it the wrong way and that the things he was doing was driving him farther away from me and our home.

He asked, "What are you doing?"

I told him some of the behaviors that were not normal for him like the spending, the drinking, the pornography, giving money to prostitutes, I said. "Why don't you see your doctor again?" I asked.

But he said, "Doctors can't help me."

I explained, "I can't help you either because I am not a doctor."

"You don't care about me."

"I do care about you and I love you which is why I want you to get help. Can't you see that?" I asked. "I love you very much, but I can't stand to see what you are doing to yourself."

The next day he called again saying that he was getting ready to leave Alabama and that he visited his aunt on the day before. He had been there all week and waited to visit her until the day before he was leaving. That Sunday night he called and asked if he could come over and spend the night.

I said, "I guess so." He got upset and said, "That's alright I want you to be sure." and that he would find somewhere else to stay.

He said, "I want to come home, but I know I did wrong." "I can't help what happened in the past, but I only have .40 in my pocket."

"How would returning home help me?"

All he could say was, "I am working.".

"Where is your money going?"

He said, "I don't know but I was paying the house note with what I am giving you from my retirement pay."

"We both worked for that money and both agreed that the retirement money would pay for the house."

"Half of it should be mine."

"You walked off and left your half."

Of course, he hung up. I don't know why I keep asking him about money because it never ends well but I just get so upset with all of this.

He called me at home and wanted me to bring his grandfather's gun to work for him as well as his pistol and his dad's rifle so he could sell them and leave town. I did not bring the guns to work, and he never did ask me if I brought them. About two hours later he called to tell me that he had cancelled our life insurance and wanted me to deposit $85 to his account each month. $85 had been taken out of the retirement check for our insurance. The next day he came into my office and said his pants were too big and asked if I would fix them for him. I said I would. He called back and said he didn't have any money and needed a place to stay for a few nights this week.

I said, "You can't just walk in and out of my life like that, we need to talk about this and what has happened."

He said, "I don't know what has happened."

None of this is making sense. What is he up to?

Franklin called before I left for work. He wanted to talk but my phone had so much static that I was having a hard time hearing him. I told him I couldn't understand what he was saying and that we should talk later. Before I got to work, he had already called my office. Shortly after I arrive, he called back and said he was getting a divorce so that I could have my freedom.

"You don't want me, and you don't want to help me. I don't want to talk to Lyle for at least 30-60 days. My whole family has put me down, I will apply for the divorce, and it should be final in 90 days. I will not ask you for anything ever again. My whole family has turned against me. No one wants to help me. I will not ask any of you for help again. I am tired of this. I am fed up; I can't take it anymore. I have a half tank of gas, I asked you if I could stay there a couple of nights so I would not have to drive over to the boat every day. All I want to do is stay in the guestroom."

He hung up the phone and did not give me a chance to respond to anything he had said. I just shook my head.

The next call came at 7:45 am on Wednesday. He wanted me to sign for a loan with household finance so he could pay off some of his bills.

"If I get the loan, I will have just one payment to make. The loan would be a lien against our house." he said.

"No, absolutely not, I will not do that."

"Put the house up for sale now so I can get my money out of it".

This time I hung up the phone on him. The nerve of him to even suggest that. Now he wants me to not even have a place to live!!

When I got to work, he came into my office, handed me the papers from the loan company, and said that he would talk to me when he got back. I don't know where he went but he did not come back for the papers.

Franklin called the next morning at 7:50 am asking if I read the papers. I had but told him I was not going to sign for a loan against the house for him or anyone else.

"I said no and that's it," I told him.

He said "OK, I will take my retirement check so that I would have money." He added, "I will close the account and have the check come to me." "You said your children would take care of you so let them take care of you. You and all my children treated me like a dog, I asked for food, and no one gave me anything. All of my family has put me down, all of you treated me like a dog". He would not let me get a word in so when I got tired of listening to the trash, I hung up the phone.

I brought the phone bill to work with me so I could give it to him because he had been making a lot of long-distance calls, and he agreed to pay for the long-distance service. I went to his office to give him the bill and he asked if he had to pay for it and I said yes. He said he didn't have any money and I reminded him that he spends more than this bill in the bars in one night. He asked me not to bring that up and I said OK. Then I reminded him that if he takes away all his salary and his retirement check he was trying to throw me out of the house and into the streets so what did he expect? I left his office and went back to work feeling sorry for myself because I was not making enough money to pay all the bills. I knew I would not be able to keep up the payments on the house. I did a lot of crying in my office, and this was one of those days that I just could not quit crying. I felt so fearful, scared, frightened, and anxious not knowing where to turn or what to do in a case like this. Later that afternoon he called me to say he was sorry. To avoid talking to him I just said "OK".

Friday afternoon he called to ask for $10.00. I asked how to get it to him, and he told me to put it in the mailbox for him to pick up. Saturday morning, I went for a walk, he came for the money but when I got back home, he was in the house. He wrote a note letting me know he was going to Walt Disney to check on a job to try and help pay of some of his debts.

25

The Final Threat

*"For out of the heart come evil thoughts, murder,
adultery, sexual immorality, theft, false witness, slander."*

— Matthew 15:19 —

I arrived at work one day and to my surprise, Franklin had made a
homemade flyer that said:

"WANTED $300 REWARD FOR ANYONE WHO COULD
EXTINGUISH THE SPOUSE ABUSE BEHAVIOR OF THIS
LADY: VIRGINIA HENDRICKS."

The poster had a 5 x 7 photo of the two of us in the middle and
at the bottom it read:

"SHE WAS LAST SEEN TRYING TO RELIEVE HER GUILT
BY WORKING WITH PARALYZED VETS OF AMERICA."

He taped these signs around the medical clinic where we both
worked. It was not a very large clinic, so everyone pretty much knew

everyone. This was not only humiliating and embarrassing but this was literally a threat posted in a federal building.

In times like these, I am reminded of my father-in-law's sermons on perseverance. I can only imagine what he went through with Franklin's mother, but sometimes this is just too much. Reverend Hendricks endured the same day to day uncertainties of who would wake up in the bed next to him since his wife was also refusing treatment for her schizophrenia. Not leaving in time cost him his life, I could have never imagined that I might face the same fate.

To top things off, one day out of the blue, I received a phone call from a social worker from an outpatient clinic telling me to get rid of the guns in the home. She also had details of where the guns were in the home, the type of guns, the description of one that would "take the head off" of a person. I was sternly advised to remove the guns NOW! At that time, we were still separated but he stopped by when he wanted, and he sometimes spent the night. I had already removed the guns after the last admission but now that things were getting more tense, I didn't know what to think anymore. Could he really be planning to end my life?

When I arrived home, he was there and wanted to come in to talk. I had already called my sisters and they were on their way over from Tampa. He was just making small talk and really did not seem to want to talk but he kept rambling. He walked back into my bedroom and when he came back, he seemed flustered. I had already given the guns to Lyle, so I knew there was nothing back there for him to find if that is what he was looking for, but I was still uncomfortable, not knowing if he had found a gun somewhere else. To my relief, the doorbell rang, and my sisters were here. He greeted them as usual, and said he had to leave. When he left, I noticed a small brown paper bag on the counter. It was full of bullets, likely used for those old shotguns that were gone. My heart started racing and I felt sick. I literally felt like my sisters just saved my life. Was he really about to take my life? I don't understand why he wanted to end my life but then again, his thinking has not made sense for a while.

My sisters stayed the weekend, and we all went to church on Sunday morning. What a timely sermon we enjoyed on "The Mystery of Peace". John 16:33 "Be of good cheer I have overcome the world". Pastor said,

"These were trying times for the disciples of Jesus Christ. The world was not ready to accept Christ. Those that did follow him had to have faith. For they, like us, were in the flesh. They also were in the world. They saw the actions the world took against Christ. They saw their Lord overcome the world. They heard his voice speaking to their soul telling them only believe and have faith. He spoke words of comfort to their soul. Hear him tell them to be of good cheer, for he had overcome the world. So could they, if they would only keep the faith.

When we speak of the world in this respect, we are speaking of people not land, not cities, or countries, but people. The world as looked upon from the standpoint of the land, sea, and sky, will not hurt us, we are not expected to overcome these, but we are to overcome worldly people. Pascal says, "Man is only a reed, the weakest in nature, but he is a thinking reed". His thought can either be good or evil. Cervantes said, "Every man is as God made him, ay, and often worse."

When Christ spoke of overcoming the world, he was referring to the scoffers, blasphemers, sabbath-breakers, sinners, wrongdoers, and the wicked. These represent the world. Ruskin once said, "He who offers God a second place offers Him no place".

My first point today beloved is that the world disguises itself. It is like Satan showing himself in the character of an angel of light; but on the other hand, he is a devil and evil doer. The Christian must be able to have enough faith and strength to face the world, to face the devil of every form, and to face a mountain of temptation. There lay before the Christian, if he hath strength to be a Christian there will be a long and necessary course of trials. But the tribulation is turned to excellent uses. Trial is the school of obedience. Trial is the means of growth of character. Trial is the training of faith. There is this sad fact of the outer life of the Christian; but the silence of the winter world witnesses to the coming life of the spring; the narrow wrapping of the narrow bud witnesses to the opening flower; the dark night witnesses to the morning; the outer struggle of the Christian witnesses to the inner life. Do you know him from within?

Let us examine some of the conditions of the mystery of peace. First, we must plainly need the forgiveness of sin. We have to stop resisting the fact that we are all sinners in need of forgiveness. Second, we must continue the onward march of a struggling soul and yearn towards God, cry out for his forgiveness, and continuously seek after forgiveness. We cannot grow weary of seeking all of these necessary steps; then for Christ unfailing of his promise remember that His word never fails. His Word is the peace and the real rest of the weary; not those that drift along with the tide. There are many Church drifters and I plead with you not to remain a drifter and don't let yourself become one.

Next I want you to understand that the Kingdom of God and his righteousness is a condition of peace. When the soul is learning to act in this life on the principle of another. To live, to move, to work, in fact, "In Christ" – then like the consistent calmness of the sunlight on the quiet summer day, then, like the majesty of stillness in the unfathomed summer night, then there is the peace. As a condition of peace, we must surrender an attractive principle and accept a severe principle of non-attractiveness. To have this peace that is so fair and that is so much needed, we must deny ourselves of some of the pleasures of the world. Stay with me now my brothers and sisters. Yes, I am telling you can't always have everything you want in the way that you want it.

Finally, let me share with you that we are led to peace I many ways. By Christ's example, By Faith in His blood, By growth in grace so Be encouraged, beloved, and know that peace is available to you. Let us pray."

Oh, how I need some peace in my life. I think this was the final threat. I now must protect myself if I expect to have any kind of future. I am going to have to make some difficult decisions. "Lord, thank you for your help as I make some tough decisions, thank you for your promised peace.In Jesus name, Amen."

26

The Hardest Season of My Life

*"I have set the Lord always before me;
because he is at my right hand, I shall not be shaken.
Therefore my heart is glad, and my whole being[a] rejoices;
my flesh also dwells secure."*

— PSALM 16:8-9 —

Monday morning Franklin called me at work and wanted me to ask one of the doctors if she knew a psychiatrist that she could recommend. I called my friend here at the clinic and she wrote down the name of a doctor and brought it to my office. I called Franklin, gave him the name and telephone number, told him to call her, and if he didn't like the way he sounded that we could get another referral. I was hoping that he would make the call and get some help, but I wonder if this was just another plot to get back home by appearing to be ready to get the help he needed.

I was getting ready for vacation to visit our daughters and he said to tell them Hi for him. I had my locks changed before leaving because I thought I might not have anything left in the house when I got back since he had been going in whenever he wanted without checking with me first. I was afraid that he would take my furniture or some other things and give it away as he had done before. I left on that Friday evening, flew to Atlanta and on Saturday morning my youngest daughter and I left for Ohio. Before I got to my daughter's house in Ohio he called.

"Virginia, why did you change the locks?" he asked. I wanted to stay there while you were gone."

"Franklin, we talk every day and I even told you where I was going and you never said anything about wanting to stay in the house.",

"I shouldn't have to ask permission to stay in my house."

I know he is going to start a fight on the phone, and I had to decide whether I want to talk to him or not, so I simply said,

"Franklin you have not lived there for over a year now and you can't keep coming and going in and out of the house as you please."

"OK, fine Virginia, have a nice trip," he said as he hung up the phone.

Now look what I have to look forward to when I get back, I thought and cleared the drama from my head so I could enjoy my time with my girls.

He finally called me again on Tuesday to repeat,

"The house is as much mine as yours and I should be able to use it whenever I want to."

"I had the locks changed because you threatened me."

"You are the coldest person I know; you don't care about me any-more," he cried.

"Franklin, you are the one that left home and the people you call friends, I don't want them in my house while I am out of town," I said.

He hung up again. I knew he was about to go into another rage and start reacting irrationally. I am sure he is taking this as rejection again, so I simply took a breath, said a prayer, and moved forward.

I returned to work the following Monday, but I didn't see him. It is so hard to walk on eggshells everyday not knowing what's coming next, but he did not show up for work that day, so it was peaceful. The next day I received a phone call from one of our friends.

"Virginia, my cousin from Ohio called me and said that Franklin called her asking to borrow $1,000.00! He said he needed the money to file for bankruptcy and for a divorce."

"Oh, really?"

I didn't know if I should be happy or sad, but I was embarrassed.

"I am so sorry to hear that he did that and I hope she told him no." I replied.

"She told him she didn't have it," she said.

"Ok, good."

"What are you going to do?"

"Nothing at this point but I guess I should start looking for an attorney."

"Well, let me know if you need anything."

"Thanks, I will. I will talk to you later."

When I saw Franklin the following day, I asked him about that, he just kept on walking, and never did answer me. The next morning, he called me at home early in the morning and asked me to bring some papers from the house. I took them with me to work but he never showed up in my office to pick the papers up. Friday morning, he called me at home again and asked if I brought the papers, he asked for. I told him they were in my car and have been there all week, but he never came to get them. When I got to work that morning, he called my office six times! On one of those six calls, Franklin tried to make me feel guilty about what was happening to him. He went on and on about how everything was all my fault, how I caused him to be the way that he is. He had absolutely no insight and the delusions were taking over again.

I said, "Goodbye dear," and hung up the phone. I can only take so much of the victim role when he clearly has a choice to help himself or not.

A few minutes later, he walks in my office and just stands there. Since he didn't say anything,

I asked, "Franklin, can I help you with something?"

"How much money do I owe you?"

"I'm not sure, maybe $30-40.".

He then asked, "Can you loan me $20? I will pay me back in 45 days."

I couldn't help but feel sorry for him. I looked in my purse and gave him $10 since I did not have $20. Monday morning, he started on my again and this time he wanted $10, the rest of the $20 I didn't have on Friday! He bugged me all day long, demanding I give him $10 more dollars. He wanted me to take off work and go to the bank to get $10 for him. We got into a ridiculous argument over why I was not going to leave work to get him $10.

I was already angry over a phone call that I got from our friend telling me about his sister calling her cousin accusing me of being the bad guy saying that I had put her brother out and took all of his money. I don't know how she came up with that story unless he told her that and she believed it. He was so good at manipulating people and will lie to get the sympathy he needs to get what he wants.

Little did his sister Marilyn know, Franklin had taken all the money out of the bank when he left home and left me with only what I had in my own name – which wasn't much. I had just opened an account in my name and have very little money in it. I decided to do that sometime after he had made a very large purchase for a lady friend of his, Sharon. I told Franklin about what his sister said about me and for him to stop telling lies on me. I had waited on him hand and foot all my life, and this is the thanks I get. He responded saying he had taken care of me because I did not go to work until after he retired from the Air Force. He acknowledged that he spent all his money in bars and tried to make me feel sorry for him by telling me how sick he was, how the mouth sores made it hard to talk. He often got mouth sores when he was depressed. I never asked his doctor about them, but they were very uncomfortable when they appeared. I guess they were kind of like canker sores, but I think they were a clue that he was not taking his medications. I reminded him that the mouth sores are there because he was not taking his medication, but he claimed he took it that morning.

The next day, he acted like I did not exist. He walked by me and didn't even speak. I spoke to him, and he just said "Hi" and kept going along his merry way.

Charles came home that weekend. He had come to see if he could talk to his dad and get him to come back home. He came into the clinic and took his dad out to lunch. After lunch, Charles came to my office. He seemed as though he didn't want to talk about how his lunch went. He said he didn't think dad was coming home and that things were worse than he thought. I had told all of his siblings that their dad was very sick, that he had quit taking his medications, and he was doing things that I didn't think he was capable of.

My mother had come from Alabama with Charles. She wanted to talk to him as well. We drove all over the place trying to find him. We finally found his car on the Navy base but did not know which building he was in. We waited there for a while. After he didn't come out, we went home, and I took her to Franklin's office the next day so she could talk to him. She told me that I better find someone else because he would not be back. He told my mother that I was rude and didn't care anything about him, and he was out having fun. He gave her the impression that he had found him another lady friend. My mother advised me to go on with my life. Franklin had made it clear that he would not be coming back to our home to live. I was the target of his anger, and he was convinced that I was out to get him. This anger was driving him to refuse proper treatment.

Next thing I knew, Franklin filed bankruptcy without my consent, and I was getting notices that I was going to have to sell the house. I had no other choice then to find an attorney and explore my options, which I knew meant divorce. This was by far the hardest decision of my life. Divorce was the last think I wanted but I felt my happy-ever-after was not going to happen. I wanted to beat the odds and fulfill my covenant to God 'til death do us part' but not at the hands of the man I love. I know that almost all marriages fail when bipolar disorder is in the mix, but I loved Franklin with all my heart. I wanted him to be happy and healthy, but I had to accept the fact that he had to want that for himself, and he had to fight for it more than me.

Being a caregiver can be hard and the impact of mental illness on a family is heavy. Although we grew up together, raised a beautiful Christian family, we couldn't survive mental illness on our own. Looking back, no one knows for sure what could have changed the ending to our story. No one can choose their genetics, but we can decide how to live with the cards God deals us. I believe faith and treatment are key. Although it has always been hard for me to talk about, I wish I had been more open about what I was trying to handle alone. Perhaps the support of my family, friends, providers, and the faith community could have made a difference for my family and for me. It certainly would have helped me not feel so alone in the fight to encourage Franklin. I didn't know or understand how to best help him and so he rejected my efforts. I know God has always been and will always be a large part of who Franklin is, but I will always wonder if he had never taken his eye off the cross maybe our "happy ever after" would have had a chance. I am happy that we both found a way to change the end of our stories and I pray that our future generations do the same.

ABOUT THE AUTHOR

Brenda Webb Johnson has a PhD in Adult Education and is licensed as a clinical social worker (LCSW). She has worked in a variety of social work roles over the past 30 years of service to the Department of Veterans Affairs. She currently lives in the Tampa Bay area. Over the years, she has intentionally avoided working as a provider of mental health services. Instead, she chooses community outreach activities seeking to help other African American families learn how to get a proper diagnosis and treatment and live successfully with mental illness the way her father has. The mental health system has indeed come a long way but there are still great challenges in getting proper assistance for those in need.

Brenda is a wife, mother, grandmother, and independent travel advisor with a passion for helping others. She is a military dependent who has been married for 30 years with two adult children and one grandchild. She enjoys new adventures, golf, softball, traveling, and of course continuous learning. Although this story is inspired by her family's journey, it is a fictional account that combines her mother's voice, her father's stories, her life experience from outreach efforts, and she prays it resonates with those who have questions and need a little push to not ignore what's in front of them. This story was written to inspire all not to allow themselves or anyone else they know to suffer in silence, to find support, and successfully live with whatever cards you're dealt in this short thing we call life.

For more information contact Dr. Brenda Webb Johnson, *Drbwebbjohnson@gmail.com, maniclovebooks.com*

www.ingramcontent.com/pod-product-compliance
Lightning Source LLC
Chambersburg PA
CBHW020333010826
48970CB00010B/644